Jonathan McDuffee Brewster

Fidelity and Usefulness

Life of William Burr

Jonathan McDuffee Brewster

Fidelity and Usefulness
Life of William Burr

ISBN/EAN: 9783337848361

Printed in Europe, USA, Canada, Australia, Japan

Cover: Foto ©Raphael Reischuk / pixelio.de

More available books at **www.hansebooks.com**

FIDELITY AND USEFULNESS.

LIFE OF

WILLIAM BURR.

BY

REV. J. M. BREWSTER.

DOVER, N. H.:

F. BAPTIST PRINTING ESTABLISHMENT.

BOSTON: D. LOTHROP & CO.

1871.

PREFACE.

———◦◦◦———

Soon after Mr. Burr's death, four years ago, the subject of preparing a biography of him was mentioned to me. In consequence of other engagements the work was deferred, but on my return to New England after an absence of several months, I determined that it should receive my first attention.

Believing the presentation of simply representative facts and incidents to be the true method of writing biography, I have found materials so abundant that it has been my constant aim to contract rather than dilute. Indebted to numerous sources for assistance, I shall make special mention of none of them, as they will all become apparent to the thoughtful reader.

Having undertaken the labor as one of love for him whose memory I revere, I have pursued it with growing satisfaction. My task being now completed, I offer this little volume to the public, hoping and praying that it may be of some service in the cause of the Great Master.   J. M. B.

Nov. 1, 1870.

CONTENTS.

FIDELITY AND USEFULNESS.

I.

THE BOY AT HINGHAM.

THE influences which contribute to form character and determine destiny are numerous. It is, therefore, difficult to decide at what point the biography of an individual should really commence. Ancestry, the time and place of birth, the social and moral atmosphere in which the early years were spent, are all entitled to be considered, and to have their value estimated. True always, these things are especially so of the case in hand.

WILLIAM BURR was born in Hingham, Mass., June 22, 1806. His parents were Theophilus and Sarah Waters Burr, and he was the seventh of ten children, seven sons and three daughters, of whom only one son and two daughters survive.

Descended from an old Puritan stock, his ancestry can be traced back through six generations, covering a period of more than two hundred years. In 1639, Rev. Jonathan Burr emigrated from England to Dorchester, Mass. Having been graduated from one of the English colleges, he had, for some time, preached in Suffolk, not far from where he was born. His, age at the time of his arrival in America, is unknown, but his career in his new home and field of usefulness was short. Settled in 1640 as a colleague with Mr. Mather, he died the year following, leaving a widow, three sons and one daughter. The names of the sons were Jonathan, who was graduated at Harvard College, John and Simon. It was through the line of the last that the subject of this biography descended, while the names of the two former seem to have been preserved in each successive generation. The family, as a whole, was noted for its longevity and numerous progeny. Theophilus Burr, the father of William, was the fourth of seven children, and died in 1835, in the seventy-fifth year of his age, while his grandfather, John Burr,

was one of ten children, nearly all of whom
lived to a good old age.

The earlier years of the present century, during
which William Burr was born and received his
first impressions, constitute an interesting period
in our country's history. Nearly twenty-five years
subsequent to the revolution, the people had, in a
great measure, risen above the burdens which it
imposed, and were enjoying the blessings of
freedom and good government. The fruits of
industry and social order were everywhere manifest. But while peace prevailed and prosperity
abounded, the public mind was not free from
disturbing influences. The federalism of Washington and the elder Adams was being supplanted
by the democracy of Jefferson and Madison. In
New England, especially, the dividing line between
what was known as the "orthodox" and "liberal"
wings of the "standing order" was being drawn,
and the foundations of a fierce theological controversy laid; while the doctrine of free salvation,
as preached by Benjamin Randall and others, was
warmly welcomed by the people. The influence
of the questions which were then agitating both

church and state, was felt, not only in the cities
and larger towns, but it also reached the rural
communities and neighborhoods.

Hingham, situated on the sea-coast, seventeen
miles south-east of Boston, was then and is still,
for the most part, a rural town. Settled at an
early day, its inhabitants were generally staid,
industrious and intelligent farmers. Containing
at first two Unitarian parishes, the political and
theological controversies which were in progress
at the commencement of the century, caused what
was known as the first or western parish to be
divided, and the Rev. Joseph Richardson, who is
now living at the advanced age of nearly one
hundred years, was settled over the more vigorous
and progressive portion. What now seem to us
minor issues, long since dead, were once live
questions, and stirred society to its very foundations. It is by means of such convulsions that
the people learn independence and self-reliance,
and from them comes strong and vigorous manhood. Had not our nation been tried in its
infancy, it could not have endured the burdens
and withstood the conflicts of later years.

* Died September. 1871.

In a house, still standing in that part of Hingham known as the lower plains or West Hingham, lived Theophilus Burr and his wife, Sarah. Moderately blessed with the things of this world, retiring in their manners and leading quiet lives, they were industrious, intelligent and highly respected, as were their ancestors who had lived in the same community for several generations. As already stated, there were born unto them ten children; and it seems to have been the highest ambition of the parents to instil into the children the principles of sound morality, and their own habits of industry and self-dependence. The sons belonging to this household, as is almost universally the case with farmers' sons, were required to labor on the farm the entire year, with the exception of two or three months in the winter, when they were privileged to attend the district school. And it may be said to the credit of most farmers' sons, that their scanty educational advantages are usually well improved, and made to contribute largely to future advancement and usefulness. The Burr family afforded no exception to the rule.

It requires no great stretch of the imagination to see these Burr boys toiling through the summer and fall, impatient of the slow progress of time, and fondly anticipating the luxury they would enjoy when the winter term of school should commence. And when their anticipations were realized, it is easy to see with what eagerness they improved the hours and moments of those winter days and evenings. Of all that numerous household no one evinced greater love for study, or was more beloved, than the frail and sickly boy, William. Indeed, the parents often cited his example to the other children as worthy of imitation.

To show how he was regarded, a story is told by the surviving members of the family, to the effect, that one day his younger brother Pyam, who is still living, visited an orchard some distance from the house, but returned without bringing his mother any of its fruit. For this act of neglect she reproved him sharply, saying, " Your brother William would not have done such a thing." This allusion to the noble and generous conduct of William in comparison with his own, cut him to the very quick, and so keenly did he feel the reproof, that it has never been effaced from his memory. It is also told of him that, though intent on saving his earnings for a special purpose, he took from them to aid his sister, younger than himself, so that she might have her wants supplied, without being under the necessity of providing the means herself. He thus early manifested the benevolence and great kindness of heart which were among the prominent traits exhibited in subsequent life.

As may be inferred from what has been already said, Mr. and Mrs. Theophilus Burr were Unitarians, and connected with the parish of which Rev. Mr. Richardson was pastor. They were regular attendants upon public worship, and carefully practiced and taught their children the great principles of Christian morality; but they claimed to have little or no sympathy with " evangelical religion." There is, however, reason to believe that Mrs. Burr, like many other Unitarians, especially of that day, lived a life of prayer and experienced the saving grace of God in her heart.

The children of these parents were " christened, "

in accordance with the custom of the " standing
order." William was in fact the first child " christened" by Mr. Richardson on assuming the duties
of his pastorate.   When quite a lad, he attended a
" catechism school," established and taught by Mr.
Richardson, at which much moral and religious
instruction was imparted.   At this school, after
the lessons were recited, the pastor often spoke
with great earnestness and emotion, weeping himself and causing the children to weep.   Thus we
get a view of one side of the religious training to
which the mind of William Burr was early subjected, — the example of a secretly pious mother
and the teachings of an honest and earnest pastor.
But there were other influences at work in connection with these things, which had a powerful
and lasting effect.

An aunt, who seems to have been an experi-
imental Christian, lived in his father's family and
took his religious training under her especial care,
and, among other things, taught him the Lord's
Prayer.   When not more than four or five years
of age, he was deeply impressed by the death of
Mr. Thomas Burr, an aged uncle of his father,

whose residence was only a few rods distant. When told that "Uncle Thomas" was dead, his curiosity was excited; and when he learned, on inquiry, what it was to die, his feelings were greatly wrought upon. He came to know, for the first time, that he too must die, as well as his father and mother, and his brothers and sisters. But he was, at the same time, made acquainted with the glorious and comforting doctrine of the resurrection, as far as his childish mind could comprehend it, and especially was he taught that the good would be happy after death. The influence of these early impressions was never outgrown, and it is quite impossible to tell what effect it must have had upon his subsequent life. Thoughts of death and of the future can not be rightly impressed upon the mind at too early an age.

When some eleven or twelve years of age, his brother Waters Burr died, aged twenty-six. This unwelcome event in the family, which occurred only a week after the marriage of Waters, caused great thoughtfulness on the part of all its members. There was, at that time, a gentleman familiarly called "Uncle Pope," a

Freewill Baptist minister, who married his mother's sister, on a visit to the family. Though among impenitent relatives, he did not neglect, as many in like circumstances often do, to speak a word for Christ, and to urge this sorrowing family to secure a hope in Jesus, the Saviour of sinners, as the only sure refuge in trouble. The words spoken found a lodging - place in the heart of William. He resolved to give himself to Christ, prayed much in secret, and, had he been aided by the prayers, sympathies and counsels of experimental Christians, he would doubtless have dated the commencement of his religious life from that time. As it proved, however, he was only a thorny - ground hearer. The fascinations and frivolities of youth choked the progress of the word of truth. It is not a little remarkable that this early religious experience, though short - lived, was the result of the faithfulness of a humble Freewill Baptist preacher, who little thought that the name of the modest, retiring and pale - faced boy, who caught every word as it fell from his lips, was destined to become a household word in the young and rising denomination with which he was connected. This circumstance should encourage the Christian laborer " to sow beside all waters."

The habits of industry and self-dependence which the boy, William Burr, had been taught by his parents, led him early to raise the question, what calling he should thereafter pursue in life. Having a strong love for study and an ardent desire to be useful, his first impulse was to go to college and become a minister ; but when he discovered that such a course was impracticable, he decided that, should the way open, he would be a printer. He soon began to lay various plans, by means of which he might realize this cherished purpose. A printer was, doubtless, what God designed he should be, and he had an important work for him to accomplish in this capacity, though the door through which he was to enter upon his future career was a long time in opening. God alone knows what preparation of mind and heart it is necessary that his servants should receive to qualify them for the work for which he has designed them. He has, however, something for them to do just as soon as they are qualified. This is a lesson which many are slow to learn and accept.

In June, 1821, the month in which the boy, William Burr, completed his fifteenth year, with high expectations, he went to Boston to search for a place in a printing office. He spent the entire day, calling at every office which he could find, but to no purpose. No apprentice was wanted; and when night approached, the words of the father, who accompanied the son, " Come, William, you had better return home with me," were heard with bitter disappointment. But his cherished purpose was not to be relinquished. In the following August he again visited Boston, with the same object in view, but his efforts were attended with no better success, and he returned home more sadly disappointed than before. It should be recollected that Boston was a small place half a century ago, in comparison with what it is now, and that even a less number in proportion were engaged in publishing. These facts will explain, in part, why a situation could not be readily found for a boy who wished to learn the printer's trade. Though disappointed a second time, the hope of realizing the object upon which his heart had been set was not abandoned.

In one of these fruitless searches for a place, he met a wealthy gentleman, who, observing that he was a mere boy, said to him: "Come and live with me three or four years, attend to the calls of my door bell, and wait upon my table. You will then have time enough to learn the printer's trade." But he was not the boy to be allured from his chosen work by such invitations.

———

At this point, the first period in the life of the subject of this biography properly terminates. The boy is, in an important sense, the germ of the man. The native qualities, manifested during the earlier years, will, under ordinary circumstances, mature and ripen during the later ones. Descended from an honored puritan ancestry, early taught habits of industry and self-reliance, manifesting a special regard for his parents as well as for all the members of the household, evincing a strong love of study, impressed with the importance of seeking the salvation of his soul, and decided in his calling for life, one could have easily predicted that the boy, William Burr, would make just what he actually became as the man, William Burr. It is to be regretted that the incidents of this period of his life can not be more fully detailed. But we have enough to afford an insight into what he really was, and his character and example are commended to the young as worthy of study and imitation.

During his life - time, Mr. Burr always maintained a strong attachment to his early home. Although his parents had gone to their resting-places, though his brothers and sisters had become scattered and some of them were no more, and though but few of his early associates remained to welcome him, there was still a peculiar charm, in the good old town of Hingham, — in its balmy atmosphere, its pleasant scenery, its delightful beach, and, above all, the familiar spot which gave him birth. He consequently visited the place as often as his arduous duties would permit, to revive old associations and to note the changes which had taken place ; and he ever took special delight in narrating incidents which came under his observation,

and in which he participated during his boyhood.   He paid his last visit to Hingham in July,
previous to his death in November, 1866.   The
Hingham of to - day is, in some respects, different from that of half a century ago.   Its villages
have increased in size, its beach has become a
watering - place, and many of its inhabitants are
believers in " evangelical religion."

II.

THE APPRENTICE IN BOSTON.

After the period of germination, there usually comes one of trial. The boy, William Burr, was destined to pass through one of peculiar severity. Apprentices, at the present day, can have only an imperfect conception of the hardships which fell to the lot of those who served in a like capacity half a century ago. Securing a place, perhaps, with much difficulty, the apprentice was usually bound to serve a master seven years. At first required to perform some of the most menial offices, his progress was watched with a suspiciousness sometimes amounting to jealousy. In addition to these things, he was often roughly treated and poorly fed and clothed.

The apprenticeship of William Burr was attended with its full share of annoyances. Twice defeated in his efforts to secure a place in a printing office, and impatient to be doing something, he served for a short time with his brother The-ophilus, who was a house carpenter in Boston, and, a few weeks subsequently, with a Mr. Wheel-wright, a manufacturer of musical instruments and umbrellas. He did not, however, fully relinquish the idea of becoming a printer, though he prob-ably would have served an apprenticeship with Mr. Wheelwright, had not a circumstance, trifling in itself though important in its consequences, oc-curred to lead him to the realization of his cher-ished purpose. The accidental breaking of a pane of glass while splitting wood caused his employer to be so angry with him that he heaped upon him much personal abuse; and the time for which he was engaged having expired, he wisely declined to remain with him longer.

On the second day after leaving Mr. Wheel-wright, he secured a place in the printing-office of Mr. George Clark. The exact time when his term of service with Mr. Clark commenced, and the time of its continuance, are unknown. It is probable, however, that the former was not later than November, 1821, and it is to be presumed that the latter was until he was of age. It was

agreed, among other things, that he should receive
his board and clothes.   Engaged now in a work
which he relished, he devoted himself to it with
great energy and perseverance, and made unusual
proficiency in mastering the elements of the art.
But at the expiration of two years, he had received only his board in Mr. Clark's family and a
single pair of shoes.   During this time he had obtained a portion of his clothing from home, and
had managed to earn the remainder by procuring
small jobs of printing from merchants and others,
which he performed before and after the usual
hours of labor.   He sometimes worked until a
very late hour, and on one occasion all night.   It
should be said, however, in behalf of Mr. Clark,
that he had failed, and was greatly embarrassed,
in his business.

Tired of this kind of treatment, as he had reason
to be, the young apprentice wished to leave Mr.
Clark and seek employment elsewhere.   His
employer objected to this, as young Burr had
now become profitable to him, and he even
refused to give him a recommendation by means
of which alone, according to an arrangement

then existing among printers, he could gain admittance to another office. But from this perplexity relief came in the kindness of two brothers of Mr. Clark, then merchants in Boston, who knew the character of the boy and gave him permission to refer to them.

Consequently he was soon able to obtain employment in the office of Mr. John Frost, then one of the largest and best printing - offices in Boston. He remained here until July, 1825, but his situation with his new employer was neither pleasant nor desirable. Frequent demands were made upon him, such as proof - reading and errand - going, as were not made upon the other apprentices, though one of them had come into the office more recently than himself. It had been agreed between himself and Mr. Frost that, after setting four thousand ems a day, he should be paid for all additional work at journeyman's prices. He therefore considered it unjust for him to spend so much time in doing work for which no allowance was made. Besides, Mr. Frost paid less for his board than for that of the other apprentices, and had at length come to owe him quite a large sum

earned by working out of his usual hours. Young
Burr had frequently sought for a settlement and
the payment of his due, but he could obtain neither. Bearing all his grievances for a long time
without murmuring, the hour came when he could
do so no longer, especially as abuse was added to
abuse.

At the close of a hot summer day, after the
other hands had left the office, Mr. Frost demanded of young Burr that he should carry proof-
sheets to an author residing in a distant part of the
city, and return and spend a portion of the night
in correcting a form which he wished to have in
readiness for the press in the morning. The apprentice respectfully declined to correct the form
that night, but said he would do it in the morning and have it ready at an early hour. To this
he received the stern reply, "You *must* do it to -
night." Mr. Frost thereupon left the office for
his home expecting, doubtless, that all his orders
would be obeyed as usual. Vividly impressed
with a sense of the wrongs which he had already
suffered at the hands of his employer, our young
apprentice determined that for once he would not

compromise his manhood, let the consequences be what they might. He accordingly carried the proof-sheets to the author as directed, and went to his boarding-place. This decision, costing him no doubt a severe struggle, proved a turning-point in his career.

As he promised, he returned to the printing office early the next morning, and was busily engaged in correcting the form when Mr. Frost came in. Angry because his orders had not been obeyed, he gave young Burr a severe reprimand. In reply to this, he said, " Mr. Frost, if you are not satisfied with my course since I have been in your office, it is best for us to have a settlement, and for me to leave." " But," said Frost, " if you leave my office, I will prevent your obtaining employment in any other in this city." " But Boston," rejoined young Burr, " is not the only place in the world."

During the conversation, however, he told Mr. Frost that if he would settle with him, pay him his due and treat him as well as he did the other apprentices, he would still remain with him. But Mr. Frost then giving him a peremptory command that he should go to work unconditionally, he refused to comply and left the office.

From some points of view, this conduct of young Burr may seem rash and willful, but those acquainted with the patience and coolness which he manifested in riper years, must know that, unless he became greatly changed, he could have been moved to such a course only by the severest provocation. But whenever a principle or his own individual honor was in danger of being compromised, he ever stood firm and abided the consequences. During his apprenticeship, he passed through a discipline which served to qualify him for the arduous duties of his subsequent career.

Having left the employment of Mr. Frost, and feeling that, with his influence against him, there would be no opening for him in Boston, he decided to go elsewhere, little realizing the extent of the trying experiences which still awaited him. Accordingly, on the next Monday morning, July 9, 1825, young Burr left Boston on the early stage for Providence, where he arrived in the afternoon. The length of the journey, the heat of the day, and a sense of his lonely and friendless condition, caused him to be weary in body and dejected in mind. He felt even more dejected at the close of the next day, which was spent in fruitless search for employment. Though he visited every printing-office in town, he could find no opening. His money was nearly gone, and, in view of his straitened circumstances, he felt that he must do something at once. In his perplexity, he went to the wharves to seek a chance to go to sea. Finding a ship soon to sail for Buenos Ayers, he was informed by the mate, in the absence of the captain that he could be employed as a sailor, if he desired it; but, at the same time, he was advised not to accept the situation. The youthful and frail appearance of young Burr called forth from this mate, who seems to have possessed much kindness of heart, the remark that sea-faring life was hard, and he would encourage no young man like him to undertake it. This opinion caused him to suspend his decision another day, but he was determined that, should he still be unsuccessful in his search for other employment, he would take the proposed voyage.

Having spent another day in fruitless effort, he was preparing, on the following morning, to go on board the vessel. At this juncture, he received a note from a journeyman in the *Patriot* office, stating that he desired to spend a short time in the country and wished to engage him to fill his place during his absence. The invitation was readily accepted, and he went to work feeling relieved of a great burden. Meanwhile, he had received letters from his friends, to whom he had written stating his condition and intentions, in which he was entreated not to go to sea, but to return home. Thus a kind providence watched over and preserved him.

At the return of the journeyman for whom he was a substitute, it being seen that he was a good workman, he received and accepted an invitation from the proprietors of the *Patriot* to remain longer. He worked for them and other parties until December, in spite of the efforts of his old enemy, Mr. Frost, who visited Providence in the meantime, and sought to procure his discharge. In December of the same year, 1825, the *Traveller* was started in Boston, and the proprietors engaged Mr. Parmenter of Providence to take charge of its printing. This gentleman was a friend of young Burr, and he invited him to return to Boston and assist in carrying on this work.

He accepted the invitation and went back to Boston, but not to make it a permanent home. He felt sure his old enemy would follow him and seek to annoy him in every possible way as long as he was within his reach. On this account he dreaded to go back to this city. It soon proved that his fears were not groundless. He had scarcely become settled in his new situation when he learned that Mr. Frost and one of the proprietors of the *Traveller* were on very intimate terms, and that the former often visited the counting-room of the latter. In view of these facts, he began to look about for employment elsewhere, and he was not long in finding it.

During the month of February, 1826, two strangers of somewhat peculiar dress and manners entered the composing - room of the office of the *Traveller*. They were close observers, and were in turn closely observed. It was soon un-

derstood that they had come to Boston in the
interest of Hobbs, Woodman & Co., Limerick,
Me., a company formed for the purpose of publishing a religious paper, and that going to the
office of the *Traveller* to obtain information and
assistance, they had been referred to Mr. Parmenter. They wished for assistance in purchasing type and other materials for printing, and to
learn of some suitable person who could be obtained to take charge of the work. Young Burr
at once became anxious and secretly hoped that
the choice might fall upon himself. He was consequently greatly disappointed on learning that Mr.
Parmenter had recommended a person of more
years and larger experience. These gentle-
men, who proved to be Elders Henry Hobbs and
Samuel Burbank, had a conference with the person recommended and made a conditional bargain
with him. After their return to Maine, however,
from some cause, he was obliged to inform them
that he could not meet his engagement. The
hopes of young Burr, who was apprised of what
was going on, began to revive ; and, having an interview with Mr. Parmenter, in due time he re-

ceived the following letter, the original copy of
of which is still in existence. The form and style
of the letter are preserved as nearly as possible:

     "Newfield, March 27th 1826.
Mr.
   Burr, Sir you being recommended as
capable of managing a Printing Press for us,
and through the medium of Mr. Parmenter en-
gaging to serve us for the sum we offered Mr.
———. Confiding in Mr. P. you being a stranger
to us, we wish you to come on, and enter into the
business as soon as may be. You will not now
be enabled to arrive by the time we set in our
letter to Mr. P. but you will arrive perhaps by
the 10th, of April, perhaps before, we shall wait
your arrival but wish it may be as soon as practicable.

  Please to call on Mr. Elias Libby, trader at
the village in Limerick, and put up with him until further directions.

  We shall expect you without fail and shall look
for a workman, as foreman, no further. A disappointment will greatly injure us.

  Please to call upon Baker & Greeb, and take
with you a cut for a *horse*. I do not know the
No. not having the specimen before me, but we
want the $5.00 cut, that which is the most ele-
gant, tell them to charge the same to Hobbs
Woodman & Co. if they request an order, exhib-
it this letter.   Yours very respectfully
        Samuel Burbank
    For Hobbs, Woodman & Co.
Mr. Wm. Burr"

With such an opening before him he was relieved from all present anxiety. Spending a year
or more at Limerick, he would be of age and at
liberty to return to Boston or go elsewhere without fear of molestation from Mr. Frost or any
one else. This seems to have been the way in
which the subject presented itself to him ; and he
little realized that he was now to enter upon a
career of usefulness which would terminate only
at his death, but so it proved. While man is
short - sighted, God is far - seeing ; and while the
plans of the one are narrow, those of the other
are vast.

From a religious point of view, the life of
young Burr during this period was far from satis-
factory. At first a regular attendant of public
worship, having often a battle with conscience, and
listening occasionally to the invitations and warn-
ings of providence and Christian friends, he at
length neglected almost entirely the house of God,
and became addicted to card-playing, dancing and
theater - going. While in Providence he attended church but seldom, and after his return to
Boston but once, and then to hear the bold and
earnest preacher, Rev. Dr. Lyman Beecher, who

was then at the hight of his popularity. As he once expressed to the writer, he was at this time a careless and thoughtless young man, having no love for God or relish for his truth. As it proved, it was well for him that he left Boston.

The little less than five years covered by this chapter constitute the most dangerous period in the life of any individual. During the transition from boyhood to manhood, there is often an inclination on the part of the individual to be the man, while he is in reality only the boy. In the case of young Burr, in addition to the usual dangers of this period, the restraints of home were exchanged for the influences of city life. Having enjoyed the benefits of a sound moral training, the reader has seen in these pages how he maintained his sense of honor, and exhibited his firmness of purpose and how a kind providence directed his steps. Of him could it be said with quite as much truthfulness as of Joseph of old,—"The Lord was with him."

Mr. Burr never forgot the experiences connected with his life as an apprentice, and he took especial delight in speaking of some of them. But a short time previous to his death, he narrated them to the writer with great fullness and minuteness. While he spoke of some things with pleasure, he mentioned others with deep sorrow. He ever manifested a due sense of gratitude that, in all his experiences during this period, his feet were, to such an extent, kept from the alluring snares of the destroyer, and that the guiding hand of his Heavenly Father was constantly over him.

III.

THE FREEWILL BAPTISTS IN 1826.

In these pages, thus far, the writer has sought to unfold the character of William Burr during his boyhood, and to present in detail some of his experiences while an apprentice. Before following his career further, the reader is invited to take a view of the people with which he was in his future life to be identified.

Prior to 1780, Benjamin Randall had removed from New Castle, a small island near Portsmouth, to New Durham, N. H. His conversion had been due, under God, to the preaching of Whitefield; and, for a time, he had been connected with "the standing order." But he was not at home with them. He soon became dissatisfied with their coldness and formalism, and especially with their method of baptism. Connecting himself with the Baptists, he was, for a time, allowed to travel quite extensively and to preach or exhort.

But it was not long before it was discovered that
he failed to preach the doctrines of predestination,
limited atonement and final perseverance, as held
by the denomination at large ; and he was consequently tried, adjudged unsound, and disfellow-
shiped. Examining afresh his position, he became confirmed in it, and continued to proclaim
the doctrine of "free salvation." His earnest and
pleasing manner attracted attention, and the message proclaimed met with a ready response from
the people, who were hungering for the bread of
eternal life.

During the year bearing the date already giv-
en, Randall organized at New Durham a small
church of believers in the doctrines which he
preached. From the seed thus planted the vine
soon ran over the wall; and in spite of some of
the greatest discouragements and the most bitter
opposition, its fruit was destined to be abundant.

Assuming at first the name of "Baptists,"
other names were applied to them in derision.
One of these, that of "Freewillers," becoming in
itself a tower of strength, was incorporated with
the original name, and from the union thus formed

is the name "Freewill Baptist." As already intimated, the distinctive doctrines of Randall and
his coadjutors were Arminian as opposed to Cal-
vinistic. They taught that Christ died for the
whole human family, though faith and repentance
were necessary conditions of salvation. As
pertains to the Godhead, they were generally
Trinitarians, but the questions which relate to
this subject do not seem to have been much discussed at first. Respecting the ordinances of the
church, they practiced baptism by immersion and
discarded infant baptism; and they held that all
true believers have a right to come to the table of
the Lord. Their system of church government,
for the most part congregational, was gradually
developed, and seems to have been modified to
meet the wants of the times. The early preachers
had neither wealth, prestige, nor worldly wisdom to
commend them, but, going forth in the name and
strength of the great Master, they told the simple
story of the cross in such a manner as to carry
conviction to the hearts of sinners.

In 1826, forty - six years after Randall organized the first church at New Durham, Freewill

Baptist churches, originating from this one church as a nucleus, existed to the number of nearly four hundred, in all the New England States except Connecticut, and in New York, Pennsylvania, Ohio and Indiana, together with the Canadas. There were more than three hundred ministers and an estimated membership of about fifteen thousand. The increase would doubtless have been much greater, had the early preachers, instead of being content to confine their labors to the rural districts, sought the cities and larger towns and boldly planted their principles in these centers of influence. As it was, however, the increase was such as to show that the hand of the Lord was in the movement and his seal upon it.

At the time to which reference has just been made, Randall had been dead eighteen years, but his mantle had fallen upon others. John Colby had, after an active and useful career as an evangelist, gone to receive his reward ; John Buzzell, who had been a co - laborer with Randall, though on the shady side of life, was exerting an extensive influence ; David Marks, the boy - preacher of Western New York, had made but one or two visits to New England; Elias Hutchins, a young preacher of deep and earnest piety, was contemplating a journey to Ohio; Jonathan Woodman, though only about twenty-five years of age, had been preaching eight years; Arthur Caverno was settled at Contoocookville, N. H., and was the only minister in the denomination receiving a stated salary; Silas Curtis was a licentiate; Martin Cheney had begun to have his attention turned to his life-work in Rhode Island, and Hosea Quinby was preparing for college. With but few exceptions the active and rising ministry of that day has passed away.

The work accomplished during this period of forty-six years was in greatness and importance incalculable. The mission of the Freewill Baptists was from their origin reformatory. Called into existence by the demands of the times, they were bold, earnest and aggressive. Calvinism, as it was then preached, and an unsanctified ministry, supported by a tax levied upon every citizen of whatever faith and order, received no mercy at their hands; while wickedness in all its forms was denounced unsparingly. External opposition had not only to be overcome, but also internal dissensions quieted, and the spirit of fanaticism which occasionally manifested itself quelled. But the thing of the greatest importance was to warn sinners to flee from the " wrath to come." Having gained a foot - hold, and being keenly alive to the spirit of the age, they were fast becoming prepared for the great work before them.

Had they erected but few houses of worship; they had done all in this respect that their circumstances would allow. Had they but few or no Sabbath schools ; neither had other denominations. Had they not engaged actively in the temperance cause; the light of the temperance reformation had not then dawned. Had they no mission societies, foreign and home; the foreign mission enterprise was then in its infancy, and every minister was himself a home missionary. Had they no education society, schools and colleges; no class of men ever felt the need of an education more. Had they not become equipped for the fight against slavery; the anti - slavery warfare had not then commenced. Had no general conference been organized; they were prepared for the work, and the next year was destined to witness its completion. It is impossible to give a correct estimate of their character without an intimate knowledge of the times in which they lived.

Perceiving the advantages to be derived from the aid of the press, the Freewill Baptists were not slow to employ this instrumentality. In 1811, Eld. John Buzzell, who resided in Parsonsfield, Me., commenced the publication of "A Religious Magazine," which was continued quarterly for two years. Its publication was then suspended until 1820, when it was resumed and continued for two years. In 1819, Eld. Ebenezer Chase commenced the publication of "The Religious Informer," at Andover, N. H., and continued it eight years. It was issued at first once in two weeks, but afterwards monthly. Both of these publications were in pamphlet form, and though their circulation could not have been very extensive, they served as a valuable means of communication between the churches and did much to extend a knowledge of the doctrines and polity of the denomination. But the want of a weekly organ was felt and recognized, and the question was often raised respecting how it should be supplied. The answer, however, was not long in coming.

In 1825, as the result of a conference between Elds. Samuel Burbank and Elias Libby, whose names have already appeared in these pages, the Parsonsfield Quarterly Meeting was consulted respecting the propriety of publishing a weekly religious journal. While the Quarterly Meeting doubted the success of the undertaking, it promised its patronage. Nine men,* however, were found ready to assume its publication, and having secured a capital of eight hundred dollars at fifty dollars a share, they issued their prospectus in January, 1826. Respecting the paper they said : "The first two pages of the paper will be devoted to religious intelligence and Christian correspondence. The other two pages to news in general, and whatever may be attractive to the candid reader." The company was legally and formally organized early in February under the

---

*The names of these nine men were, Henry Hobbs, Jonathan Woodman, John Buzzell, Samuel Burbank, Elias Libby, Andrew Hobson, Joseph Hobson, Mark Hill and William Davidson, all ministers, except Dea. Joseph Hobson. Of these only Woodman, Libby and A. Hobson survive.

name of Hobbs, Woodman & Co., and Elder
Henry Hobbs was chosen chairman, and Elder
Samuel Burbank, clerk. During the same month
Messrs. Hobbs and Burbank visited Boston in
the interest of the company, and, as already stated,
young Burr was employed to go to Limerick and
take charge of the printing. Henceforth, for a
period of forty years, the history of the Freewill
Baptist denomination and the life of William
Burr were to be closely interwoven.

The reader is invited to turn from the view of
the Freewill Baptist denomination as it was and
glance at what it is. From 1826 to the present
time, there has been a period nearly as long as
the one from the organization of the first church
by Randall to 1826. During this time, the work
so auspiciously begun by the fathers has been no-
bly carried forward by those who have come after
them. While the fundamental principles of the
denomination have remained intact, its churches
have been planted in twice the number of states,
and have increased from less than four hundred to
nearly fourteen hundred, its membership has

increased from fifteen thousand to nearly seventy thousand, and its power and facilities for good have increased in a corresponding ratio. In proof of this, there may be cited the character of its churches, not only in the rural districts, but also in the larger towns and cities ; its Sabbath school work, scarcely second in importance to the preaching of the gospel ; its missions in India and among the Freedmen, in which its spirit of benevolence and consecration has been manifest ; its Theological School, which has done so much for the culture of its ministry ; its two colleges in regular operation besides others in embryo ; its preparatory schools of a high order and its Printing Establishment scattering its publications broadcast through the land. Indeed, the progress of the denomination has been commensurate with that of the nation. With especial pride can it refer to its excellent system of doctrines and its church polity, its catalogue of sainted dead and its noble record in the warfare against American slavery.

IV.

Returning from our digression, we will now resume the narrative of young Burr where it was interrupted, at the close of the second chapter.

There is something grand and significant in the Scripture account of the journey of the youthful Jacob, from the home of Isaac and Rebecca, to the country of Laban. His doubts and forebodings, his experiences during the night at Bethel, with his vows and resolutions, have not been peculiar to him. They have, rather, constituted a part of the mental history of many a young man who has gone out into the world not knowing whither he went. It would be strange if young Burr did not have thoughts and feelings similar to those of Jacob, as he left Boston for Limerick to assume the responsibilities which awaited him at the commencement of what proved to be his life - work.

The letter summoning Mr. Burr to Limerick

was written on the 27th of March, and he left
Boston on the 6th of April. In those days of
slow locomotion, not more than a week could have
intervened between the reception of his letter and
his departure. But this was doubtless a week of
activity. He must settle with his employers,
make the needed preparation for leaving and the
journey, say good-bye to his acquaintances, and
perhaps make a flying visit to Hingham to see his
parents and receive their blessing. Taking passage for Portland in a packet, which was then by
far the easiest and cheapest way that he could
reach that city, he arrived after a stormy course
of nearly three days, the greater part of which
time land could not be seen. Starting from
Portland in a wagon, and encountering the bad
roads of the season, at Buxton he was obliged to
take a sleigh for the remainder of the journey.
Dragged thus through mud and snow for thirty-
six miles, he reached Limerick just at dark, and
stopped with Eld. Elias Libby as he had been
directed.

Limerick was then a beautiful country village
of several hundred inhabitants, enclosed by hills,

midway between the ocean on the southeast and the Ossipee mountains on the northwest. It contained, among other things, a single hotel, two lawyers' offices, half a dozen stores, a chaise and harness manufactory, several shoe - shops, three churches and an academy. One of the most enterprising business men of this village was Eld. Elias Libby, who also served as pastor of the Freewill Baptist church. It was he who, when a printing - office was wanted for the new paper, invited the company to come to Limerick and occupy rooms which he would furnish either free or at a moderate charge. Situated thirty or more miles from Portland and remote from the great mail routes, this place afforded but few facilities for the publication of a weekly religious newspaper. But, in spite of all obstacles, the enterprise was destined to succeed.

Mr. Burr found everything pertaining to his future work in a chaotic state. While a company had been formed and editors appointed, none of the men engaged in the enterprise had any practical acquaintance with the work which they had undertaken. The task before him appeared formidable. Respecting his own early experiences at Limerick, Mr. Burr said, in an article which appeared in the *Star* of April 4, 1866, and which was the last article of any considerable length which he wrote for its columns,—" Arriving at Limerick, he found in the room which had been prepared for an office, a few boxes of type and some cases, and, stowed away in one corner, an ' old - fashioned' Ramage press, which looked as if it might have descended from the days of Faust. There were neither fixtures, furniture, nor models of what was requisite. He proceeded to make plans of what he wanted as best he could, and a carpenter was employed to manufacture them. The type was distributed into cases, the old rickety press set up, inking-balls made (for that was long before the days of rollers), a couple of young lads, — one of them now Rev. P. S. Burbank, of Danville, N. H., — put under a course of instruction in the art of printing ; and, on the 11th of May, 1826, the first number of *The Morning Star* was issued. The sheet was quite small compared with its present size, though it was as large as many other papers of that day. The number of subscribers was less than five hundred, the names of some of whom are still to be found upon our subscription list, though a large majority of them, with Elds. Buzzell and Burbank (the first two Editors), Hobbs and Davidson and Deacon Hobson, of the Association, have finished their earthly career, and are now, we trust, inhabitants of 'the better country'. Subscribers rapidly increased, and, by the end of the first volume, had become sufficiently numerous to pay all the expenses of publication."

Between Boston and Limerick, and the large and well - furnished office of the *Traveller* and the humble one of the *Star*, the contrast must have been great. But it was equally great to him in other respects. Trained under Unitarian influences, and though attending the Congregationalist church in Limerick, his daily associations were largely with the Freewill Baptists, and he sometimes attended their meetings. Says Rev. O. B. Cheney in *The Freewill Baptist Quarterly* for Oct., 1857, — "After he (Mr. Burr) had been in Limerick a few weeks, a F. Baptist Quarterly Meeting was held there. Much had been said

about the approaching meeting in the place, and
great preparations were made for it. As he had
never attended a meeting of the kind, he felt no
small degree of curiosity in regard to it; — the
more as a number of F. Baptist ministers were
expected to be present, and he had never seen but
two or three. At length the day of the meeting
arrived. It was a beautiful May morning. A
multitude of people assembled, as the Quarterly
Meeting embraced a large territory. The meeting was held in the old Baptist meeting - house,
standing on the hill overlooking the village. It
was one of the 'old-fashioned', two - story, barn -
looking houses, very large, with galleries, and only partly finished and plastered. Burr took his
place in the gallery, in front of the pulpit, upon
one of the rough seats which had been fitted up
for the occasion; and as he looked down upon
the men occupying the pulpit, the altar and the
front pews, ministers of the gospel, some of
them young, others venerable in appearance
by their whitened locks and peculiar dress; and
as he listened to their fervent prayers, their spiritual songs, their powerful preaching and earnest

exhortations, he could only silently repeat : 'These men are the servants of the Most High God, which show unto us the way of salvation.'" Suffice it to say that this meeting exerted a powerful influence in leading him to seek his personal salvation and inclining him to the views of the F. Baptists, though he did not date his conversion until nearly two years later.

At the commencement of the publication of the *Star*, the force in the office consisted of the Junior Editor, Eld. Samuel Burbank, then one of the younger and better educated ministers in the denomination, Mr. Burr, the printer, a part of whose work was doubtless to instruct Mr. Burbank in the art of newspaper - making, and, as already stated, two boys as apprentices, — one of whom was Alva Quinby and the other he who is now Rev. P. S. Burbank. At the request of the writer, Mr. Burbank has furnished a statement of the experiences of those early years, which is now given for the benefit of the reader. He says :

"The office of *The Morning Star*, during the first years of its existence, was a large, square room with its furniture and fixtures, — a veritable printing - office, containing a small hand, Ramage press, with stands and cases, over which William Burr presided, aided by two boys. Here one might have seen us in our every day rig, as type - setters, or pressmen, or what not. On printing days Burr and myself worked the press. The Editor's little, cosy sanctum was on the same floor, within which we all went for 'copy'. During the three years of my apprenticeship, some changes occurred in the working force of the office. Quinby left; Irving Favor and two other boys became apprentices, and I came to be what I have heard Mr. Burr call me,— his 'oldest boy', and, for those three years his most intimate co - laborer.

"Mr. Burr, when he came to Limerick, though less than twenty years of age, was, as we regarded him, an accomplished gentleman, of pleasing manners and most amiable disposition. He soon and easily made the acquaintance of the leading young men in the village, nearly all of whom attended the Congregationalist church, the largest and most popular in the village. The

Baptist church was small and a little at one side, while the Freewill Baptists worshiped in a hall in the third story of a building owned by Elder Libby. Ordinarily Mr. Burr attended the largest church. During the first two years everything went smoothly in the village and the office. Many were the visitors who came to see the wonderful operation of printing, among whom were many of our ministers. I could tell, as a distinct remembrance, that in the large basket which carried our mail to the post - office, the Wilton package of *Stars* was the largest that went to any town. Hubbard Chandler brought us in the most subscribers, and Arthur Caverno sent the plainest and neatest manuscript communications that came to the office.

"The third year brought a glad change to us and the village. God sent a religious awakening, which filled the place, swept the entire town, and pervaded all three of the societies. Early in the year 1828, Eld. Clement Phinney, then a revivalist well known in Maine, came to Limerick and preached in our church several Sabbaths and evenings. He was accustomed to see souls con-

verted under such circumstances. But here the
result was only the partial awakening of the
church. Not a sinner had chosen Christ. Dis-
heartened, Father Phinney took the stage for
home. The next day, to the great surprise of
all, Samuel L. Julian, the leading man in one of
the carriage shops, was present at a church conference. Immediately after the meeting was
opened by prayer, he arose and said, 'I feel like
a stranger in a strange land, and I ask the prayers
of Christians for my poor soul.' He soon found
peace in believing, and in the precious revival
which followed, he has sometimes been spoken of
as 'the first convert'. Others requested prayers
in the same meeting. A messenger was dis-
patched for Father Phinney, who returned and
preached several weeks longer with great power.
Mr. Burr, who was a friend of Julian, was one of
the early converts in the revival. In the following months each of the three societies in the
village received large accessions. Among the
fruits of the revival were several who became
ministers.

"Converts' and inquirers' meetings began to be

held, soon after the commencement of the revival, in Julian's carriage shop or in the *Star* office, and these private meetings gathered new attendants, either as seekers or new converts, as the revival progressed. When Burr had attended several of these meetings, and I had not, one day while both of us were setting type, not far from each other, Burr said to me, abruptly but very quietly,—' Burbank, *What do you think of religion?*' I said,—' I suppose it is important.' He said,—' That is not what I mean. I mean, what do you think of *seeking* religion.' I answered,—' I suppose I ought to.' He added,— ' I mean to. I think these Christians enjoy something that I do n't, and though I never felt myself to be so great a sinner as some, I think religion to be a good thing, and I mean to seek it, and I hope you will, too.' I was already a private inquirer, and, not long after this conversation, we were both hoping in Jesus.

"This conversation indicates something of the character of the man. In business or religion, calmly and deliberately, he asked *what was duty*, and did it. He concluded that *religion* was the

supreme good, and sought to procure it.   In all
the social meetings of that revival, as in all the
remaining years of his life, he was ready to ' stand
up for Jesus'.   He was a humble Christian and a
sincerely devoted Freewill Baptist, to whose
heart the interests of the denomination were always
dear.   And who of us, living or dead, has done
more for it?"

In connection with the revival under the labors
of Father Phinney, a volume, entitled, " Persua-
sives to Early Piety," by Rev. J. G. Pike, of
England, then just published, found its way to
the *Star* office, and was seized and read by young
Burr. Its pungent truths carried conviction to
his heart, and the seed sown in due time re-
sulted in a harvest.   In October he was baptized
by Eld. A. Bridges, and united with the Freewill Baptist church.

The conversion of *Brother* Burr, as he was
ever afterwards called, determined his subsequent
career, and exerted an important influence upon
the future of the denomination.   Previous to this
event, he had decided to leave Limerick and return to Boston, at the close of his second year's

engagement. He would then be of age, and had no more to fear from his old enemy, Frost. He had notified his employers to this effect, and they, having given up all hope of retaining him, had engaged another printer to take his place. But now, animated by a new purpose, he was desirous of identifying his interests with those of the young and rising denomination which he truly loved, and to the principles of which he was becoming strongly attached. The contract between the proprietors of the *Star* and the printer whom they had engaged, was, by mutual consent, annulled, and the services of Mr. Burr continued.

The year 1828 witnessed another event in the career of Mr. Burr, second only in importance to his conversion. In June, he was married to Miss Frances McDonald, the fifth daughter of the then late John McDonald, of Limerick.

Mr. Burr had been steadily gaining in the confidence of his employers from the first, but now, having become an active and experimental Christian, this confidence strengthened, and many looked to him as the one in whom the hopes of the denomination, as they had reference to its publishing interests, centered. In the spring of 1829, at the commencement of the fourth volume of the *Star*, the position of both Office Editor and of Publishing Agent were tendered him; but while he accepted the latter, he declined the former. As a reason for this, he urged his youth and want of acquaintance with the denomination; and in this he exhibited his characteristic modesty. He performed, however, the duties of both positions, as Elds. Buzzell and Burbank had become but little more than editorial contributors. In fact, Mr. Burr had, during the previous three years, performed much of the labor which usually devolved upon an Editor, such as proof-reading, making selections, and the like.

Meantime, changes were in constant progress in the firm which commenced the publication of the *Star*. Some who composed this firm disposed of their stock and dropped out, while Mr. Burr, who showed his faith by his works, invested in it his carefully saved earnings. In May, 1832, the firm of Hobbs, Woodman & Co., disposed of its property to a new firm, known as Hobbs, Burr & Co., which was to continue the work of the old firm. The property of the new firm was divided into twenty-three parts or shares. Of these, William Burr owned fourteen shares, Henry Hobbs, John Buzzell, Samuel Burbank and Joseph Hobson, two shares each, and Robert Cole, one share. According to the terms of agreement, no person was to own more than fourteen shares of the stock, and the copartnership, which was formed for ten years, could not be dissolved without the votes of eighteen shares in its favor. These conditions may be regarded as significant. But as it is proved, this copartnership continued only until the following October, when the paper was sold to the denomination,—a result accomplished largely through the instrumentality of Mr. Burr. One year later, the *Star* and the interests connected with it, having outgrown Limerick, were removed to Dover, N. II., where it still continues to emit its rays.

Limerick remains a beautiful village, with its town hall, academy, three churches, and its plain residences occupied by a busy people. The build-

ing in which the *Star* was printed has long since
been removed, and others have taken its place.
The disinterested traveler looks upon it as a neat
and prosperous village, but to a denomination of
Christians it is endeared as the spot that gave
birth to *The Morning Star*, and as once the
residence of one of its leading benefactors,—
WILLIAM BURR.

V.

During a portion of his life, Mr. Burr kept a journal, but how long he did this is not known. All that has been found of it is comprised in a few scraps which appear to have been written during the late spring and early summer of 1830, the period covered by the preceding chapter. The fact that this is the only thing which he left that partakes of the nature of an auto - biography, and the interest which many readers are likely to feel in the character of his religious experience, have seemed to warrant giving it special prominence.

None can read the following pages without a strengthened conviction that the individual, of whose mental and spiritual history they form a part, "walked with God" and sought to maintain constant communion with him.

"WEDNESDAY AND THURSDAY, *May* 26 and

27.—Attended the Gorham Quarterly Meeting at Buxton. The reports from the churches were not very refreshing except in a few instances. Eld. Chandler preached in the afternoon of the first day. On the second day, A. M., Eld. Elijah Shaw preached an excellent discourse. It was indeed a strengthening one, it is believed, to many of God's dear children. In the afternoon, Eld. Andrew Rollins preached, followed by many feeling exhortations from several other preachers. During this Quarterly Meeting my mind has been considerably unsettled a part of the time. None, or at least but little, of the preaching seemed to suit my case exactly. But I hope I gained some ground. The weather was very pleasant and the collection of people very large. Happened to meet with Bro. Capples at this meeting, who informed me that he was going to Limerick. Stayed Wednesday evening at a Mr. Wells's, where I found kind treatment and had the privilege of praying with the family, but had but little access to the throne of grace. Indeed, I seemed almost insensible while attempting to call upon the name of the Lord. Lord, show me the worst of my case, and give me a knowledge of my duty and grace to perform it!

" FRIDAY, *May* 28.—Arrived home last evening from Q. M., and found all well. The Lord had been pleased to preserve our lives through the short period we had been absent, for which I tried to thank his name, although it seemed to be a mere lip service. O Lord, soften my heart, and let me feel true penitence! To - day have had much of the world in my mind, and but little have my thoughts been on eternity. Oh, who shall deliver me from this cold and stupid frame of mind, but the Lord? To him will I raise my voice, for his mercy alone can reach my case. This evening a prayer - meeting is to be held at Bro. Burbank's, at which Bro. Capples is expected to be present. Lord, give him a meek and lowly spirit!—The weather at the present time is exceedingly dry.

"Attended prayer - meeting last evening, and the Lord was in our midst. It was a solemn time, and I gained a victory over myself in resisting the devil. This afternoon one of my -brothers (Elijah) called on me, from Hingham. He came entirely unexpected, and brought news that all my relatives in that place and vicinity were in the enjoyment of health when he left home. Was glad to receive him, being the first visit I ever received from either of my relatives, since I removed to this place, over four years ago.

" Sabbath, *May* 30.—My brother being with me, and not being a professor of experimental religion, and being necessarily obliged to converse with him considerably on subjects which were not religious, my mind gradually departed from the contemplation of religious things and from a devotional frame, so that, before the day closed, I found my soul in a barren condition indeed, although I seemed, as I thought, unwilling that this should be the case, and strove against it; but I have no doubt that the cause was found in withdrawing my mind from its appropriate duties on this holy day. O Lord, I need thy gracious assistance in this time of trial!—Eld. Burbank, Bro. Capples and Eld. John Buzzell preached at the meeting-house. It is to be hoped that some good will result therefrom.

"Monday and Tuesday, *May* 31 *and June* 1.—My brother still remains with me. Have conversed with him much on religion, but find that he still holds to morality as all-sufficient, and received no benefit myself from the conversation. I therefore concluded, as I am not likely to do him any good nor to receive any myself from him, that I will not introduce the subject to him again while he is present with me.

" Wednesday.—My brother started for home

this morning. I accompanied him as far as Waterboro', where I took my leave of him, perhaps no more to meet him till the Judgment of the great day. Have I cleared my skirts from the blood of his soul, if this should prove the case? Of this I am doubtful. The subject was displeasing to him. He thought me too much concerned. 'The soul,' he said, 'would be well enough, if we did not trouble ourselves so much about it.' I did not like to displease him, for fear that his visit would not be agreeable, and excused myself by supposing that I could do him no good. I fear that thereby I have been unfaithful to warn him of his danger as I should. If this be the case, I pray thee, O Lord, to forgive, and I will endeavor to be more faithful in time to come. Oh, increase my faith, of which I am now almost destitute !

" Thursday.—Attended meeting this afternoon at half - past five, at Stimpson's school - house. But few attended, and it was rather a dry time. Bro. Capples was present and seemed to be engaged. Tried to exhort my fellow creatures to seek an interest in the Saviour's blood, but it seemed to me to be of no avail. . . . .

" Friday, *June* 11. — Started for Sandwich, where the Y. M. was held. Arrived at the place about half-past eight, and found several brethren already there. Enjoyed myself very well on my journey, being in company with Bro. N. Burbank. We took dinner at Effingham with Mr. Marston, and were very kindly entertained. After dinner we had a little praying time and were much refreshed. This evening I was made acquainted with a number of brethren from different parts of N. H., whom I never before met, and saw a number of old acquaintances. On retiring for the night, the throne of grace was very appropriately addressed by Eld. Wm. Buzzell.

"SATURDAY, *June* 12. — This morning I arose at a very early hour and repaired to the grove near Bro. Ambrose's, where I stopped, and tried to thank the Lord for his goodness to me, but in consequence of the scattered situation of my thoughts, from being in a strange place and seeing so many strangers, I did not experience that access to the throne of grace enjoyed at other times, although I felt that I was doing my duty. About nine o'clock I went to the meeting - house where the meeting was to be held, and heard some very feeling remarks from Eld. Place, on the necessity of brethren assisting their preachers more. He stated as his belief that, in many places in N. H., the people were awaking to this duty and coming forward in support of it. He knew of several who were desirous of bestowing a part of their earthly substance for the benefit of the ministry, and said he believed, if temperance should increase as fast for five years to come as for two years past, that many who had been hitherto unable to contribute anything to this object, would be able to do considerable. The report from the Q. M's were, on the whole, very encouraging. During the meeting, I heard sermons from Elds. Flanders, Woodman, Caverno and Buzzell, some of which were awakening to sinners and edifying to the saints. I tarried on Saturday evening at the north part of the town, with a man who was not a professor of religion, but he appeared very serious and treated me and my companion with great kindness.

"SUNDAY.—Heard Eld. Woodman in the forenoon, and Eld. Caverno in the afternoon. Eld. C. preached a very practical discourse from these words, — 'Nay, Father Abraham, but if one were sent unto them from the dead, they would repent.' Towards the close there were but few present that were not seen to weep. Some broke out in loud sobs.

"On Monday, about nine, the brethren who had met from different quarters began to disperse to

their respective homes. The sight was very
affecting. Here we had been together for several days, and had taken sweet counsel with each
other; but now all these enjoyments are over,
and we are to part, many of us to meet no more
on the shores of time. Lord, help us so to live that
we may meet around thy dazzling throne in the
kingdom of heaven!

"We started about nine, arrived at Bro. Hodg-
don's, in Ossipee, for dinner, and at Bro. Mason's,
in Effingham, for supper, where Eld. Woodman
preached, and it was a good time. After meeting, a man by the name of Watson, who formerly lived in Limerick, came and took hold of my
hand, and, after the usual ceremonies, asked me
with a faltering voice, if I would not call on him
before I left the place. I replied that I would.
He had, while at Limerick, lived rather a sinful
life, and also after he removed to Effingham, up
to this time. Seeing some signs of penitence in
him, I followed him to his house, when he informed me that he felt himself to be a lost sinner,
shedding many tears. I tried to encourage him
to go to Jesus, and united with his family in
prayer. I saw him the next morning, and he
appeared to be still bent down under a load of
guilt. The Lord help him to seek till he finds.

Tuesday, about noon, I arrived at my dwelling and found all well.

"WEDNESDAY AND THURSDAY. — Enjoyed some happy hours and endured some dark seasons. Feel resolved to try to arise through divine assistance to a newness of life, to live more exemplary and prayerful. Lord, help me so to do!

"FRIDAY, *June* 18. — Eld. Bridges preached at the meeting-house at five o'clock, P. M., and some exhortations were delivered at the close. Five came forward for prayers, among whom was H. J. Libby, who had been, for some time, trying to build upon Universal Restoration. Apparently the Lord is about to revive his work and to carry it on with mighty power."

VI.

FROM LIMERICK TO DOVER.

The last number of *The Morning Star* printed at Limerick bears the date of Oct. 31, 1833, while the first number printed in Dover bears the date of Nov. 14. One number only was suspended in consequence of the removal. This suggests active work, especially in view of the fact that a hard road of nearly fifty miles lay between Limerick and Dover.

It is one thing to give the date of an event, while it is quite another thing to determine the causes which produced it. Mr. Burr never believed that Limerick was a suitable place for the publication of the *Star*, or that the enterprise would attain the highest success in that locality. With each year the conviction strengthened that, should the *Star* become a great denominational paper, its removal would be only a question of time.

But the execution of new measures often de-

mands new men. The first proprietors of the
Star were all, or nearly all, residents of York
County, Maine. One object had in view in commencing its publication was the local advantages
to be derived from it ; and, while some of these
men may not have been very decided in their opposition to removal, it could have been hardly expected that they should favor it. But at this
time, as at other times when God has a work to
accomplish, he had in readiness the means of its
accomplishment. Two men appeared upon the
stage, whom Mr. Burr found very efficient and
valuable co-laborers. For a portion of the time,
one or both of these men was even more prominent than himself, though he was more than any
other one, the originator of the new movement.

The name of Eld. David Marks, known as the
boy-preacher of Western New York, has already
appeared in these pages. Born in Shendaken, Ul-
ster Co., N. Y., in 1805, and removing with his
parents, a few years later, to Junius, Seneca Co.,
he was converted while a mere child, and commenced preaching at the early age of fifteen.
Feeling that " the woe was upon him," he traveled,

on foot, on horseback, and then with his two horses and covered carriage, far and near, and delivered his plain and simple message with such unction and power that the conversion of hundreds and thousands was the result. At one time he was in Western New York, a few weeks later in New England, and a few weeks later still, he had returned to New York and had gone to Canada, from which he returned to make a journey to Ohio or another one to New England. For those days of slow locomotion, he was as well-nigh omnipresent as a mortal could be. Though his early educational advantages were small, he was a diligent student, reading and writing as he traveled from place to place; and, possessed of the devotion of a monk and the activity of a Jesuit, his influence was extensive and his power for good immense.

In 1828, while Eld. Marks was attending the second General Conference at Sandwich, N. H., his preaching attracted the attention of an intelligent and thoughtful young man of retiring manners and skeptical tendencies, whose parents were members of the Society of Friends. His conver-

sion followed, and he and Eld. Marks became intimate friends. This young man was Samuel
Bedee. Born in Poplin, now Fremont, N. H.,
in 1799, he had been a resident of Sandwich since
the age of seventeen. "Though," to use the
language of Eld. Marks in reference to him, " he
enjoyed small advantages of attending school, he
gave his mind to study from childhood, and even
while engaged in other pursuits, he was diligently employed in gaining knowledge. He studied
the sciences, the Latin language, and paid
some attention to the Greek, and gave himself to
very extensive and critical reading. He looked
deeply into things, treasured up vast knowledge,
and finally became one of the most correct English scholars." The articles from his pen, as
they afterwards appeared in the *Star*, showed
him to be a pungent and accomplished writer.
These three young men, Burr, Marks and Bedee,
of nearly the same age, were attracted to each
other, and united their efforts in the accomplishment of a work, which, doubtless, neither of
them could have accomplished alone.

The practical acquaintance of Mr. Burr with

the work of publishing and the interest which he
had felt, since his conversion, in the welfare and
progress of the denomination, led him to under-
stand something of its wants and to devise means
to supply them. Knowing, among other things,
what the Methodist " Book Concern" was doing
for the denomination in whose interests it was
established, he readily conceived that similar advantages would accrue to the Freewill Baptists
from a similar institution. He pondered the matter long and well; and, at length, he gave
a few brief hints in reference to the subject,
in the *Star* of Feb. 9, 1831. It will be
sufficient to reproduce a single paragraph from
the article. He said :

" Other denominations of Christians are all
alive; their forces, well marshaled, are in the
field; and they are making every exertion, and
using every means to build up Zion and dissemi-
nate their doctrines. Not only are their preachers engaged in the work, but they have applied to
the press for her powerful aid. Witness their numerous periodicals, their Tract Societies, and
their ' Book Concerns.' The enemies of the cross,
too, have taken to their assistance this mighty en-
gine, and are thereby scattering their baleful and
deleterious doctrines far and wide. And shall

not the Freewill Baptists also have the benefit of
the press? Yes — We have it already, and let
us be more careful in the future to secure its advantages."

As might have been expected, this article arrested attention. One after another expressed
his views through the columns of the *Star* in advocacy of the establishment of a "Book Concern."
Among these was Mr. Bedee who, at the sugges-
tion of Burr, wrote a series of articles over an
anonymous signature, in which he set forth the
necessity of a "Book Concern," and the advantages to be derived from it in an able and convincing manner. The name of the writer of
these articles was known to no one except
Mr. Burr, until the death of Bedee, when he
considered himself absolved from the secrecy laid
upon him and revealed it. At this day, it would
seem strange that it was deemed necessary to present an elaborate argument in favor of such an
undertaking, but these men were then doing pioneer work. They were treading upon a *terra
incognita*. Some looked upon the new movement with suspicion, while others doubted its financial success.

At first, Eld. Marks devoted himself almost solely to the procuring the immediate conversion of sinners. But more recently, he had come to feel deeply in view of the wants of the denomination, and especially its educational wants. He was consequently greatly interested in this discussion in the *Star*. The idea of the "Book Concern" met his views, and he corresponded with his friend Bedee respecting it. The first step taken was to secure the endorsement of the General Conference, which met at Wilton, Me., in Oct., 1831. This body, however, was cautious in its movements. While it said, — "We believe that such an establishment, suitably encouraged and supported, would contribute as much to usefulness in our churches, and aid as much in spreading Christian knowledge in the world, as any other single course of measures that we can under the present circumstances pursue," it had no funds with which to undertake such an enterprise on a large scale. Consequently it could only appoint Eld. Marks as Book Agent until the next General Conference, with authority to publish for the Conference such books as it should direct, hold himself responsible to the Conference for his acts, and be himself responsible for all contracts made. A Publishing and Advisory Committee, consisting of H. Hobbs, S. Bedee and Wm. Burr, was also appointed, " with instructions to direct the Book Agent to publish, for and in behalf of the Conference, such books as they might deem suitable and expedient to be so published, and to advise with him relative to the sales." Of this Committee Mr. Burr was chosen Secretary. Such was the origin of the Freewill Baptist Printing Establishment. From this humble beginning, it has grown to its present dimensions.

But this step being taken, others must soon follow. With *The Morning Star* published at Limerick in the interest of its proprietors, and the " Book Concern" owned by the denomination with its head quarters at the same place, there were two institutions, between which there was liable, sooner or later, to be rivalry and friction. Besides, the time would come when the " Book Concern" would want a paper of its own, which would be the official organ of the denomination. Foreseeing these contingencies and desirous that

the unity of the denomination should be preserved,
Mr. Burr decided that the wiser course to be per-
sued was for the denomination to purchase the
Star; and, consequently, he, with other proprietors, proposed its sale. The proposition was accepted by the General Conference, held in Mere-
dith in Oct., 1832. Thirty - seven hundred dollars was the sum agreed upon, but as the Confer- .
ence had no funds at its disposal, and the "Book
Concern" was already in debt two thousand
dollars as the result of its first year's operations
in publishing, the benefit of the credit system was
given to the fullest extent. The subscribers of
the *Star* then numbered about one thousand and
six hundred. The Book Agent was continued in
office, and the Publishing and Advisory Committee was increased by the addition of the names of
Hosea Quinby, Silas Curtis and D. P. Cilley.

After the purchase of the *Star*, it was nomi-
nally published by Eld. Marks as Agent of the
"Book Concern," while he continued to act in
that capacity. Traveling, preaching and circu-
lating books, he came to Limerick only when his
duties called him there. Mr. Burr still superin-

tended the printing and had the immediate over-
sight of the editorial and financial departments of
the paper. Mr. Bedee seems to have spent some
time in Boston in the interest of the " Book Concern," and wrote freely for the *Star*. Before the
first year after the purchase had expired, the number of subscribers had increased to two thousand
and seven hundred, and the removal had been
virtually decided upon. In August, Marks wrote
to his friend Bedee, saying, among other things,—
" We have almost endless perplexities in publishing books in the country. . . . Bro. Burr and
myself are about discouraged. We think the removal of the office the only remedy'; the sooner the
better, unless we should incur censure."

Previous, however, to the session of the Gen-
al Conference, held in Strafford, Vt., in Oct.,
1833, the Publishing Committee took formal action upon the subject, and presented to that body
substantially the following statement :

" Several disadvantages have been experienced
by our Book Establishment on account of its un-
favorable location. Being situated in an interior
country town, those facilities for publishing, printing and distributing books and papers have not

been possessed, that a place of more business, and of more central situation would have afforded. Some particular inconveniences that have been suffered, we would state for the consideration of the Conference."

Then followed six specifications, and the Committee concluded by saying that these inconveniences could be remedied by the removal of the establishment to some place where intercourse with other parts of the country would be easier and mail accommodations better.

"The General Conference," said the *Star*, "took the above statements into consideration, and, after making such inquiry and examination as it saw fit, in relation to the probable advantages and disadvantages of Limerick, Portland, Dover, Boston, Providence and other places named for a new location, agreed "That the Printing Establishment be removed to Dover, N. H., as soon as convenient." But why Dover was selected, in preference to Portland or Boston, does not appear from any statement on record. It was probably chosen, however, as a compromise between Limerick and Boston, and in consequence of its central position among the New England churches and the advantages which the place itself afforded. Mr. Burr once told the writer that this selection was in accordance with his own preferences, and it does not appear that he ever regretted the choice made.

Dover, from that time to the present, the headquarters of the publishing interests of the Freewill Baptist denomination, is situated on the Cochecho river, twelve miles from Portsmouth, and sixty - eight from Boston. Within its limits the first settlement in New Hampshire was made in 1623, three years after the settlement of Plymouth, Mass. Twelve years later, Major Richard Waldron settled at Cochecho Falls, at the head of tide water and now Dover proper, and in process of time, both the business and the population centered at this place. The inhabitants suffered severely during the Indian wars, in which occurred the famous Waldron tragedy in 1689, the story of which will continue to be told in connection with the history of Dover, for generations to come. In 1833, the town contained nearly six thousand inhabitants, and was the second in population in the state. It had, for twenty years,

been a manufacturing town, and its four cotton
mills and its printery gave employment to fifteen
hundred people, and afforded the great stimulus
to its business.   It had water communication
with Portsmouth, and it was the center of no less
than sixteen different mail routes, by means of
which it had direct communication with Boston,
Lowell, Concord, Portsmouth, Saco, Portland,
Augusta and a large number of other places.
Here were then published three papers, the *En-
quirer*, the *Gazette*, the *Unitarian Recorder*,
two of which are still in existence. " The Land-
ing" was then the Central square, and Main and
Cochecho Streets, the Franklin square of to - day,
while the "old Court House" answered for that
time for what the City Hall is now.   Daniel M.
Christie had been in the practice of law in the
place some ten years, but though diligent and laborious, his reputation had not been achieved.
John P. Hale had, a few years before, opened
his office, but ten or twelve years must pass before he was to be animated with his great life -
purpose ; and the wealthy, gray - haired men who
now walk the streets, were then the young and

rising men of business.   There were eight religious societies in the place, viz.,—The First
Congregationalist, (the second in the state), the
Friends', the Methodist, the Universalist, the
Freewill Baptist, the Unitarian, the C. Baptist
and the Catholic.   The Freewill Baptist society
or church, of which Eld. N. Thurston was then
pastor, had been organized seven years and had
a membership of one hundred and thirty.   Its
house of worship, on the corner of Chestnut and
Brick streets, now devoted to another purpose,
had been erected a little more than a year, and
all the interests of the church were in a prosperous condition.—It was in this place that Mr.
Burr, then twenty - seven years of age, was destined to spend the remaining thirty - three years
of his useful life.

The " Book Concern," including the *Star*,
found its home at first over a store on Central St.
just south of the bridge, and everything was
soon in running order.   But until the commencement of the new volume, in May, there were for
Mr. Burr six busy months.   He had to become
accustomed to his new position and relations;

his co-laborers were, a part of the time, sick, in consequence of which his own burdens were increased; the Committee for the compilation of the first edition of the "Treatise," of which he was a member, had three sessions, two of which were of several weeks duration; and what brought anguish to his soul, his friend Bedee, who had been appointed to take the editorial charge of the *Star*, and was to come into the office at the commencement of the next volume, sickened and died.

For several weeks, during the months of January and February, the editorials of the *Star* seem to have been almost entirely from Mr. Bedee's pen.

Among the last articles which Mr. Bedee wrote was one entitled, " Slavery and Abolition," in which he took the ground, that, though slavery was an evil, it was one for which the North was equally responsible with the South, denounced the course of emancipationists and counseled the exercise of moderation and charity. After writing this article, it would almost seem that he laid down his pen, never to take it up again. His triumphant death, which occurred on the 28th of

March, was deeply and sincerely mourned as a denominational calamity. But if this article foreshadowed what the course of the *Star* would have been, in reference to the " Great American Conflict," had he lived, seeing things from our standpoint, we are led to say,—" God's ways are not as our ways." The death of Mr. Bedee left a vacancy not to be easily filled.

During the next year and a half, there does not seem to have been anything in Mr. Burr's career particularly new or striking, apart from his usual routine of duties. But important changes were soon to follow.

VII.

THE PUBLISHING AGENT.

In these pages, thus far, it has been the aim of the writer to treat of the career of Mr. Burr in a continuous narrative, in which it has been sought to present the different phases of his life. In this chapter and several chapters which follow it, another course will be pursued, since, subsequent to the point now reached, Mr. Burr's duties became so numerous and his life so diversified, that the method hitherto adopted becomes unwieldy. The new method will become apparent as the reader proceeds.

At the General Conference, held at Byron, N. Y., in Oct., 1835, Eld. Marks resigned the agency of the "Book Concern." Wearied by his excessive labors in traveling, preaching and attending to business, he had decided to leave New England and return to Western New York, to seek rest in a more retired sphere of action. For

the service which he had rendered the " Book
Concern" during the four years of his agency, he
had charged only a little more than seven hundred dollars, besides one hundred and fifty dollars for traveling expenses, although his own
private property was held, during the time, for
debts contracted. The Conference expressed itself satisfied with the service rendered and accepted his resignation.

The Conference then appointed a Board con-
sisting of eleven members, viz.,—Wm. Burr,
Silas Curtis, Daniel P. Cilley, Jacob Davis,
Enoch Place, Joseph M. Harper, Samuel Burbank, Trueman Carey, Elias Hutchins, Seth C.
Parker and Charles Morse, to be known as "The
Trustees of the Freewill Baptist Connection,"
who should assume the responsibilities of the
Book Agent and manage the affairs of the " Concern." Among the duties devolving upon the
Board were the employment of the printer and
the appointment of the Editor or Editors of the
Star, and the preparation and publication of such
books as it should deem expedient. These Trustees were also directed to obtain from the Legis-

lature of New Hampshire, an act of incorporation
for their Board, as soon as it could "be done
with prudence and safety."

From the report of the Book Agent made at
the General Conference, it appeared that the
" Book Concern" was at this time over six thousand dollars in debt, while about this sum was
regarded as collectable on what was due from subscribers and agents ; and the assets of the "Concern" amounted to some more than four thousand
dollars in addition. But as subsequent experience proved, the estimate made of what was collectable was too large, so that it is not probable
that if the affairs of the " Concern" had been then
closed, it could have much more than paid its
debts. Where the blame for this state of things
was chargeable is very obvious. Said the Publishing Committee in its report to the Conference,
written by Mr. Burr,—" As to the future prospects of the *Star*, the Committee are of the opinion that with prudent management, a continuance
of the patronage which it now receives, and
punctuality on the part of subscribers in making
payments, it will be able to pay its debts in the

course of two or three years. As will appear
from the account of debts now due, there is most
to be feared from neglect in some of the subscribers to make payments." Among other things,
this Conference voted that the *Star* be enlarged,
which was the fourth enlargement since the commencement of its publication.

The first meeting of the Trustees, held in Dover
soon after the General Conference, was a critical
and important one. No act of incorporation having been secured, the Trustees were required to
give to Eld. Marks a bond of indemnity, and become personally responsible for the debts of the
" Book Concern." There was consequently a
nervous anxiety on the part of some of the members of the Board, who feared a failure. But
something must be done. Mr. Burr was requested to take the Agency. Knowing the actu-
al state of things better, probably, than any one
else, he shrank from the responsibility. At
length, however, he consented to accept the position proffered, provided an effort be made to raise
five thousand dollars by a loan for three years,
and that, to secure this loan, the property of the

"Concern" be divided into one hundred shares, one of these shares being given as security for every fifty dollars borrowed. In this way a little more than half of the proposed sum was raised, much of which came from members of the Board. As an example of the difficulties attending the situation, it is stated that soon after the adjournment of this first meeting, one who had signed the bond given to Eld. Marks, demanded that Mr. Burr should take his name from the bond or call another meeting of the Board. But declining to do either, he gave the person mentioned his own private bond, assuming all his liabilities in addition to his own. Mr. Burr felt that he had put his hand to the plow and could not look back. The enterprise must and should, under God, succeed.

The nine years which followed 1835 were years which tried men's souls. The financial crisis of 1837 and '38 came on, and the bankrupt of 1841 with all its attendant evils followed in its trail. The Trustees of the Establishment applied, year after year, to the Legislature of New Hampshire for an act of incorporation, but their application

was as steadily refused. Some of the Trustees declined to become personally responsible for the
debts, as required by the General Conference,
while others resigned. The enterprise had to
encounter a storm of opposition from within and
without the denomination; but the Agent, sustained by the counsels and sympathies of such
men as Harper, Place, Curtis, Hutchins and
Woodman, braved the storm and came safely into port. Other establishments of the kind went
down, but not the *Star*. Respecting what had
been accomplished during these years, Mr. Burr,
in his official report to the General Conference,
held in Plainfield, N. Y., in Oct., 1844, said:

"When the Establishment came under its present management, nine years ago, there was a debt
standing against it of $6,222,48. This debt has
now been entirely canceled, with the interest
which had accrued upon it, (including the
money borrowed on stocks,) land has been purchased, and a neat and commodious building
erected for the use of the Establishment, at an
expense of about $2,000; cash is now on hand to
the amount of $670,86, and the demands of the
Establishment have increased from $9,373,70 to
upwards of $30,000, all of which is the proper-
ty of the denomination. The subscription list of

The Morning Star has also been increased
about two thousand, notwithstanding all the efforts which have been made against it. When
we look back upon this period, and consider the
difficulties we have encountered, the opposition
we have met, the cares, anxieties, and perplexities
we have endured, truly we can say, ' Hitherto
the Lord hath helped us.' To his name be the
praise.' "

Such was the success of the Establishment during the first nine years of Mr Burr's agency, and
well could the Conference say, through the chairman of the Committee on " The Printing Establishment," Rev. D. Waterman,—" The conductors
have had many severe trials to encounter, without
funds and with heavy liabilities, and, exposed to
jealousies arising from local and personal feelings,
they have toiled on, discharging their arduous
labors with faithfulness and ability, which has secured to them the approbation of the denomination generally and the respect of the Christian
community."

The building referred to in the report of Mr.
Burr was erected in connection with the Washington St. Freewill Baptist society, the upper part of
which it owned and occupied as a place of wor-

ship. In describing it, he said,— "It is about seventy feet long and forty - six wide. Its walls are of brick, and it contains a composing room, a press room, a book room, a counting room, a room for a bindery, a paper room, and a cellar under two - thirds of the building, which is a convenient storage." It was completed and entered in Nov., 1843, and the apartments which it furnished were occupied by the Establishment until after the death of Mr. Burr. It was at the Conference in 1844 that direction was first given for the appropriation of five hundred dollars, annually, to each of the Benevolent Societies.

From 1844 to 1865, the Printing Establishment enjoyed continued prosperity. It obtained its act of incorporation in 1846, when it ceased to be called the " Book Concern." The *Star*, enlarged and improved in 1851, had its subscription list increased from seven thousand to about eleven thousand, new and valuable books were added to the list of publications, the places of those Corporators who had died or resigned were supplied by other and serviceable men, the annual appropriations were made to the Benevolent societies, together with occasional donations to institutions of learning,—including three thousand dollars to Hillsdale College,—safer and better methods of doing business were adopted, and the crisis occasioned by the recent conflict was safely passed. In October, 1865, Mr. Burr attended the General Conference, held at Lewiston, Me., as it proved, for the last time. As learned from his official report and other sources, the assets of the Establishment amounted to sixty thousand, three hundred and eighty - five dollars and twenty - two cents. Of this sum, thirty - eight thousand dollars were invested in a permanent fund. Since 1844, when the Establishment became free from debt, at least forty thousand dollars had been contributed from the earnings of the Establishment to the various benevolent enterprises of the denomination. *Not a single dollar had been donated* to the Establishment from any source.

Having stated thus briefly the difficulties that were surmounted and the successes that were achieved by the Printing Establishment, under the leadership of Mr. Burr, it remains to point out the means by which the results reached were accomplished. It may be said, in the first place, that it was by the practice of the strictest economy. In everything which pertained to the Establishment, Mr. Burr exercised as much care and solicitude as in any private interest. He saw that nothing was wasted. He felt that the minutest article belonging to the office, even to each type and rule, belonged also to the Lord, and that he was placed as the keeper over it. At first he employed, as far as practicable, apprentices as compositors, because that, with the exercise of proper care, this kind of help was the cheapest; and, to save still more, he boarded them in his own family. The salaries paid were all small. His own salary was at first only three hundred and fifty dollars, then five hundred, then seven hundred, and then for a few years a thousand dollars. Only for the last two or three years before his death did he receive more than the last named sum. It would have been raised oftener, but he refused to have it done. In this respect he was willing to place himself upon a level with his co - laborers in the ministry.

To economy, Mr. Burr added practical knowledge of his work. He knew the quality of every article purchased, its value and uses, whether it was paper, type or ink. A practical printer himself, he knew also the quality of work. He had every individual in his employ under his eye; was he inefficient and wasteful, he knew it; was he competent and interested, he knew that also. Having once proved a man, he was slow to release him and put an untried one in his place. At the time of his death, his pressman had served him thirty years, his clerk twenty - one years and his foreman eighteen years. His compositors, principally ladies, had each served for a term of years. .

There were also thorough business qualities. Mr. Burr was prompt, exact, reliable and honest. He knew men and understood how to deal with them. In business circles, wherever he was known, his name was a synonym of integrity, and wherever he went, as a representative of the Establishment, he carried with him the influence of his great power of personal character,—and the more so as he advanced in years.

Again, Mr. Burr exhibited a large amount of forethought. He had constantly an eye to the future. Whatever was to be done was undertaken in its season. When material of any kind was wanted, it was usually in readiness. If a crisis approached, he sought to be prepared for it. For instance, when our national struggle came, the financial safety of the Establisment was to him a thing of momentous interest. He saw at once that, with the supply of cotton from the South cut off, the price of paper must advance beyond any former precedent. He brought the telegraph into requisition, and in a single day, while other publishers were apparently asleep, he had saved the Establishment, or the subscribers of the *Star*, thousands of dollars, for he was thereby enabled to afford the paper at its old price until near the close of the war. At the Conference in Lewiston, in his remarks accompanying his financial report, he said :

"From the above statement it appears that the profit arising from the publication of the *Star* for the past three years amounts to $7906,04, or about $2635,00 a year. But had it not been for the fortunate purchase of large quantities of paper at prices prevalent previous to the war, just before the great advance in price, and taking advantage of the market since, and generally purchasing when prices were at the lowest point, the amount, instead of showing a profit, would have exhibited a considerable loss."

Still again, Mr. Burr constantly manifested a zeal for the interests of the Establishment, amounting almost to jealousy. He was constantly on the alert to guard against everything which was liable to militate against its welfare. His characteristics in this respect may be seen from speeches which he made at the General Conferences, held at Hillsdale, Mich., and Lewiston. On the former occasion, the proposition was made to appropriate three thousand dollars from the fund of the Printing Establishment to aid Hillsdale College to endow a professorship of Biblical Literature. The following is his speech at that time as reported in the *Star*:

" W. Burr was exceedingly sorry that this resolution had been introduced. He was not opposed to the Institution at Hillsdale, but wished it well, was glad of its prosperity so far, and hoped it would continue to thrive. But he was decidedly opposed to making appropriations to this or any other Literary Institution from the Printing Establishment. . . . Other denominations in founding a Printing Establishment, have solicited and received large donations from their membership, but ours started penniless and has never received one contribution to the amount of a single dollar from any source, but is constantly paying out for the benefit of our benevolent objects. We have only about $19,000 as a permanent fund, while other similar establishments have hundreds of thousands, and regard these sums—immense compared with our little capital— as indispensable to the prosecution of their work. In view of the recent falling off of the subscription list of the *Star*, the probable continued loss on the publication of the *Myrtle* and *Quarterly*, and the increased and increasing price of paper and other printing materials, we can reasonably expect nothing more of the Establishment, while the war continues, than to hold its own and meet its expenses. Should it come to this, as there is a fair prospect that it may, what will become of our Missions, with our contributions necessarily diminished, and no funds in the Establishment to fall back upon, or to borrow in case of necessity, as they have often been obliged to do? But for the aid they have received from this source heretofore, they must have inevitably suffered, and I do not know what they possibly could have done. In addition to this, the Education Society has been dependent upon the Establishment for

$500 a year, towards the support of our indigent students, whom God is calling to the work of the ministry, and who are endeavoring to qualify themselves for the more efficient discharge of its important duties. If this appropriation should cease, to what source can it look to supply the deficiency?"

After considerable discussion the resolution was adopted with the understanding that this action should not be a precedent for the future. The professorship was named the BURR PROFESSORSHIP.

At Lewiston, three years later, when the proposition was before the Conference to dispose of some of the funds of the Printing Establishment in a similar manner, Mr. Burr made several speeches in the course of the discussion. His views were substantially as follows:

"He thought that the funds of the Printing Establishment should be allowed to accumulate until it was properly endowed. He wished the *Star* established upon a permanent basis, that it might continue to be published and exert a saving influence after he was dead. Large funds were also needed in the future to pay for the writing and publishing of books, a work which he hoped would soon be undertaken, and for other legitimate purposes of the Institution. Compared with other Institutions of the kind our fund is quite small. It was an Institution of a similar charcater with the American Tract Society, the Methodist Book Concern, the American Baptist Publication Society, and the like. Who ever heard of Literary Institutions applying for and receiving aid from them? In reply to a statement of the last speaker that we had precedents for making appropriations to our Literary Schools, he said that if we had done wrong heretofore, it was no reason that we should do so again. He had always opposed the appropriations because he believed them wrong. For these years he had had to stand, as it were, with a *club* in his hand, at the door of the treasury of the Printing Establishment to keep its funds from being scattered. To appropriate the funds of the Establishment to any but strictly religious objects, he believed would be robbing God's Treasury."

The touching emphasis with which he uttered these closing words, together with his solicitude of manner, produced a marked impression, and will long be remembered. He carried the Conference with him, gained his point, and established a principle. But, knowing that some were disappointed at the result, if not aggrieved, he called an informal meeting of the Corporators present, and, after consulting with them, employed a brother to introduce into the Conference resolutions conceding in part that for which the minori-

ty contended. These resolutions were passed
unanimously. In this act he manifested his
characteristic generosity.

———

In a career so full and round at every
point as was that of Mr. Burr, it is difficult to
tell in what he excelled, but it would, perhaps,
be making no invidious distinction to say that he
was more at home in the field of finance than
elsewhere. The fruits of his labors here will
long be manifest. The Printing Establishment
will ever stand as the monument of his labors in
this department, and his ideas of economy, business and general management will continue to
exert a wide influence. It would be difficult to
estimate the indebtedness of the denomination to
him in this one particular alone.

VIII.

EDITOR OF THE MORNING STAR.

From the commencement of the publication of the *Star* at Limerick, many of the duties usually performed by an office editor, such as reading proof, making selections, and, to some extent, the correction of manuscript, devolved upon Mr. Burr. As already stated, in 1829, the position of office editor was formally tendered him, but while he declined to accept it in name, he performed nearly all the duties pertaining to it. At one time there was a prospect that he might be relieved from this part of his service, but the death of Bedee blasted the hopes entertained.

At the meeting of the Trustees, held immediately after the General Conference in 1835, Mr. Burr was formally chosen, not only to the office of Publishing Agent, but to that of Office or Resident Editor of the *Star*. In reference to this subject, there soon appeared in the *Star* the following article, which was probably from the pen of Eld. Marks, or some other member of the Board of Trustees aside from Mr. Burr. But the question respecting the authorship is not essential :

"EDITORS OF THE STAR.

"By this week's *Star*, it will be seen that it is to be published hereafter by a Board of Trustees appointed by the General Conference, instead of being issued in the name of an individual. The Trustees have determined that it shall be hereafter edited in the following manner : Five brethren are to be engaged to furnish one column each (weekly) of original matter, designed for editorial. Brother WM. BURR is to fill the editorial columns from the articles thus furnished, make the selections and arrangement, correct and prepare communications from correspondents for the press, &c. He will also write as he has formerly done, such brief editorial articles and notes as he may judge necessary and his other numerous duties may permit.

"Doubtless there will be some inconvenience in this manner of filling the editorial columns, because the writers will be, for the most of the time, absent from the office where the paper is published. But it is thought the good taste and judgment of BRO. BURR will make amends for this, especially as this method will be likely to secure a greater amount and variety of editorial

articles than would be furnished by a single edit-
or.   This has been the plan on which the *Star*
has been edited for eighteen months past.   When
it was adopted, the Publishing Committee did not
intend to publish the signatures of the writers,
yet they designed to be able themselves to know
the author of each article by a very small figure
which the printer was to affix to each one's piece.
But the curiosity of our patrons has become so ur-
gent to know the meaning of these little figures,
that the Trustees have resolved that it shall be
published.

"The writers were chosen eighteen months
since, and their pieces are numbered according
to the ages of the authors.   Thus, number 1 was
affixed to the writings of Eld. ARTHUR CAVER-
NO ; number 2, to the pieces written by Eld. D.
MARKS ; number 3, to those of Bro. PORTER S.
BURBANK ; and number 4, to such as were furnished by Bro. J. J. BUTLER.

"The same brethren have again been elected
as editorial writers, and their respective pieces
may be distinguished by the same figures as formerly.   In addition to these, Bro. ENOCH MACK
has been elected, and will probably furnish a column a week, over figure 5."

As was anticipated, the curiosity felt was for
the moment allayed, but there is no evidence that
the *Star* was, subsequent to this revelation, more
valuable or accomplished more good.   Truth
should be received and valued for its own sake,

rather than in consequence of the instrumentality by means of which it is imparted. Far less estimate should be placed upon the vessel than upon the treasure it contains.

In making this arrangement, the Trustees little thought that it was to continue substantially the same for nearly thirty years. While some of these first writers soon ceased to furnish articles, others were added to the list, so that there are found, during the above named period, nearly twenty different names. Two of the first four, Burbank and Butler, continued until the very last. After a few years, the small figures were dropped, and the initials of the writers substituted. Subsequent to 1856 or '57, the articles appeared without signatures, except in cases where an article contained some personal reference to the writer or gave expression to views which the Resident Editor did not endorse. The principal reason for dropping the initials was that the paper might give the appearance of having greater unity in its management.

As was expected at the outset, this method on which the *Star* was conducted gave variety and ability to its editorial columns, but it had also its disadvantages.   Besides throwing a large burden of responsiblity upon Mr. Burr, in connection with his other duties, it occasioned some friction and annoyance. Residing in different parts of the country, two or more of these writers were liable to furnish articles upon the same subject, and the Resident Editor was called upon to choose between them.   Entertaining sometimes different views of a subject, they were also liable to controvert each other, and thus mar the unity of the paper. There was also danger that the questions of the day might be discussed a week or two after they ceased to be of public interest. Mr. Burr met and skillfully managed these difficulties until May, 1864, when he procured an assistant, who relieved him of much of his editorial labor, while he retained most of his editorial responsibility until his death.   But so numerous had his burdens then become that any relief was felt and val- ued.

Mr. Burr never assumed the large responsibilities entrusted to him from choice, but from necessity. He repeatedly expressed the desire that some one might be chosen to aid him in his work. But once only did the General Conference express its views in reference to the subject. This was in 1856, at Mainville, Ohio, when instruction was given "the Corporators to take into consideration the propriety of appointing an Assistant Resident Editor, to share in the editorial labors of the Establishment, and perform such other duties as they may direct;" and this was done, "in view of the increased and rapidly increasing business of the Printing Establishment, and the liability of serious embarrassment in case of failure in health or otherwise, on the part of our present worthy and excellent Editor and Publisher." Notwithstanding this instruction, the Corporators, after considering the subject more or less seriously, for five or six years in succession, were unable to make a selection. At a meeting held three or four years previous to his death, the question had been discussed and a further postponement was suggested. Mr. Burr objected, saying at the same time, with a tremulous earnestness, "I must be relieved from this burden of responsibility, for I *must have time to care for the interests of my*

soul before I die."   "Never," says one of the
Corporators, " did I hear words fall from his lips
which impressed me more powerfully."   The
whole subject of procuring an Assistant was then
left with him.

While Mr. Burr wrote but few elaborate editorial articles, the shorter notes in the paper were
nearly all from his pen ; and when occasion required, it was evident that he was not wanting in
ability to defend his position or to assail an opponent.   In 1836, soon after he became the Agent
of the Printing Establishment, he published in
the *Star* a lengthy article in which he gave instructions to Book Agents.   In the course of the
article, he named the distinctive doctrines held by
the Freewill Baptists, and included the doctrine of
" total depravity."   To this one of the Fathers in
the ministry took exceptions, and wrote a somewhat spirited article in reply.   He commenced
thus :

" In your remarks to the Agents of *The Morning Star*, January 27, you had occasion to mention the distinctive sentiments of the Freewill
Baptists ; and among others you mentioned
' total depravity.'   You say these principles of the

gospel are held among us, almost without a dissenting voice. Is it possible? Have we come to this? What! the Freewill Baptists hold this as gospel truth, that man is naturally, totally depraved, wholly inclined to evil, and defiled throughout, soul, spirit and body, and yet boast of free agency?"

Then followed more of the same sort, making two - thirds of a column in all. Mr. Burr took time to reply, and when his reply appeared, it filled nearly three columns. It can not, therefore, be reproduced here. But his method of treatment can be given. In the first place, it was important to inquire what is meant by the term "total depravity." It was possible his correspondent might mean one thing by it and he another. He then showed what he understood the denomination to believe in reference to the subject, — the total extinction of the spiritual life in man,—and quoted from the language of Eld. Randall, whose authority had great weight in those days, in proof of the tenableness of his position. He then cited the teachings of the Scriptures to substantiate the correctness of this position. His argument was skillful and convincing. After finishing the body of the argument, he said :—

" From these Scriptures it is plain that man, by nature, is totally destitute of the spiritual life —is spiritually blind and dead, and that totally. And being in this state, he is incapable of seeing or understanding the things of God's spiritual kingdom, and does not possess within himself, independent of the Spirit of Christ imparted to his soul as a *gracious* interposition, any means or faculty or power by which he could know and love and obey his Maker.   Yet the natural faculties of the soul or the understanding are not destroyed,—they still possess a degree of vigor ; the *perception of natural* things, the *will* or faculty of choice, the *imagination*, the *judgment* or reasoning faculty, the *affections* in their relation to natural objects, *hope* and *memory*, &c.,— all these faculties are inherent to our nature and exist in the soul independent of the influences of redeeming grace.   But the utmost vigor of all these faculties, unaided by Christ, could never enable their possessor to know or love God, or enjoy the things of this spiritual world,—no more than a blind person can discern, distinguish or enjoy colors.   So distinct is the natural soul from that spiritual life which God breathed into it at the first, and which, since it was destroyed by transgressions, is now imparted by the Spirit of Christ."

The following, which appeared in the *Star* some eight years previous to his death, shows how he was accustomed to deal with the statements of others which he regarded as incorrect :

" The *annual increase* of the Methodist Episcopal church
alone, leaving out the South, is more than twice as much as the
entire Freewill Baptist denomination, *though both started
about the same time.*"

" The above sentence occurs in the reply of
Zion's Herald to our New York correspondent
some two or three weeks ago. We think it contains two errors.

" 1. In regard to the annual increase of the
Methodist church,· &c. . . . . Deducting the
' probationers,' therefore, we find 55,859 left as
the net increase of the church, which, instead of
being 'more than twice as much as the entire Freewill Baptist denomination,' lacks 437 of being as
many as were reported by our churches in June
last.

" 2. The second error is found in the last
clause of the sentence quoted from the *Herald*
' *though both started about the same time.*' The
first Freewill Baptist church was formed in New
Durham, a small interior town in this state, by
Eld. Benj. Randall, in 1780. It was very small
and feeble. There were associated with Randall,
at this time or soon after, two or three other men
who had, with him, but recently commenced hold-
ing meetings. Randall and most of his early coadjutors possessed more than usual natural abilities, great piety, zeal and self-denial ; but none
of them had received the advantages of a liberal
education. They were emphatically men of one
book, the Bible. This they searched diligently,

with a determination to adopt its doctrines and directions, wherever they might lead, and that they came to correct conclusions so far as the fundamental principles of the gospel are concerned, as well as on most minor points, we sincerely believe. But, owing to the peculiar circumstances that surrounded them, on one subject of great practical importance they unfortunately adopted erroneous views, viz., *the education and support of the ministry.* This they strenuously opposed, which proved a great obstacle to their success. Believing it wrong to receive pay for preaching, they were dependent on the labors of their own hands for the maintenance of themselves and families. Hence, they could attend to their ministerial duties only on the Sabbath, and such time during the other six days as they could spare from their secular pursuits. Laboring under these disadvantages, it is not strange that they made but little progress, —that, at the end of ten years (1790), their number of members did not exceed four hundred, with but eight ordained ministers,—nor that, in 1800, they had but forty-eight churches and thirty ministers. A quarter of a century later than this, they did not probably number more than 15,000 members and 300 ministers, only eight or ten of whom, as near as can now be ascertained, devoted themselves entirely to the work of the ministry, a majority of the rest preaching only on the Sabbath. Down to this period (1825) the labors of the ministers of our denomination had been mostly confined to the states of New Hampshire and

Maine; and in these two states we number about as many as the Methodists.

"Let us now take a glimpse at the rise and progress of Methodism. It commenced in England in 1739. Its founder, John Wesley, was one of the most remarkable men of the eighteenth century. Besides being endowed by nature with a most capacious intellect, he had been thoroughly educated in literature, science and theology at the University of Oxford, one of the very first Institutions in the world. Some of his early ministers, also, were men scarcely inferior to himself. Still, the progress of Methodism in England was nearly as slow as was that of our denomination in America; for, in 1770, thirty-one years after its commencement, it numbered less than thirty thousand, with only 121 lay itinerants, and as many local preachers.

"Methodism was introduced into the southern part of this country about 1764, sixteen years before the first Freewill Baptist church was formed at New Durham, and for a long time was under the fostering care of the English Methodists. The Freewill Baptists had no such powerful and efficient aid. In 1766, a company of Wesleyans, from Ireland, established the first Methodist church in the city of New York. Among them was a local preacher, who administered to them the word of life. Two years after, says Stevens's Memorials of Methodism, to which we are indebted for these facts, a society of not less than one hundred members had been formed in Philadelphia, through the labors of Capt.

Webb. The next year Mr. Wesley despatched to their assistance two of his preachers. In two years more (1771) the laborious Asbury arrived, accompanied by Richard Wright. Asbury, says Stevens, was providentially designated as the leader of American Methodism. His vigorous and energetic mind gave it system and impulse everywhere. At his arrival, the aggregate membership could scarcely have exceeded six hundred, but in less than two years after, 1,160 were reported to the first Conference (July 4, 1773). Methodism had scattered its germs in five states. In 1784, only four years after the formation of the first F. W. Baptist church, it had increased to nearly 15,000 members and 83 preachers ; and five years subsequent, ' the spiritual host was more than 43,000 strong, led on by nearly 200 devoted itinerant evangelists. Eleven conferences were held that year, in almost as many states.' At that time our denomination numbered less than 400 members, and not more than six or eight ministers."

As already intimated, Mr. Burr's chief labor as an editor did not consist in writing editorials, but rather in correcting communications, making selections, and in controlling the columns of the paper. In all these departments he exercised much skill and judgment. During his editorial career, especially the first part of it, a large number of the original communications, as they came to the office, were very imperfectly prepared. Some of them had to be rejected outright, while others were corrected, abridged and improved. To do this work and, at the same time, not to give offense, was perplexing. Parties to difficulties in churches and Quarterly Meetings often wished to express their views of the questions involved, through the *Star*. His policy was to exclude all communications of this class, as far as possible. The following letter is expressive of his views of the subject, and is, at the same time, suggestive of his caution and wisdom. The letter itself will explain, in part at least, the circumstances under which it was written :

" Bro. ——— :

My object in delaying to publish your ' Card' hitherto has been to keep the details of the matter out of the *Star*. I do not think it will be of any advantage to you or to the cause of God to have them published, but detrimental to both. Other denominations do not, and in my opinion ought not to spread such matters before the public. Neither should we, and the only way to prevent it is to confine our publications to official documents or action. If your 'Card' is published, the Q. M. will, no doubt, wish to be heard in defense of their action, and you will probably wish to rejoin, and where will it end? You say that very many brethren think you ought to be heard. Will you please give me their names? I have no personal feeling in the matter, and wish to do what is right, but I have not yet seen the first brother who advises the publication. The matter is still under consideration, and I shall not come to a final conclusion till I have opportunity of consulting our advisory committee, which I have not yet had in regard to your 'Card.'

Yours Truly,
" WM. BURR."

In making selections, he did not always inquire what article had the greatest literary merit, but rather what would best meet the intellectual and spiritual wants of the readers. When examining his exchanges, he would often say,—"When I find an article which interests me, I am quite sure it will interest others also." For his course in the performance of the duties already specified, he was but once publicly assailed. . This was before the General Conference of 1844, when, after a long and animated discussion, so complete and convincing was his defense, that he was sustained with only a single dissenting vote, and that given by his assailant.

Mr. Burr's editorial career was chiefly distinguished by firmness and discrimination in the advocacy of the great moral questions of the day. Previous to 1835, the *Star* had become committed in favor of missions, home and foreign, Sabbath schools and an educated and consecrated ministry and membership. It continued to speak in behalf of these things, and, in the character of its advocacy, it not only kept pace with the increasing light and knowledge of each succeeding year, but it also sought to lead the way in the adoption of better views and the employment of more efficient measures. It never uttered an uncertain sound, and its opinions always carried weight.

But the *Star*, under the editorial management of Mr. Burr, was *pre-eminently distinguished* for its opposition to American slavery. Silent in regard to this subject during the first seven years of its existence, taking then the position of an apologist for slavery, during the year 1835 it became bold and pronounced in its opposition to it. If Burr and Marks ever held the views of the subject advocated by Bedee, it was not long. During the same year in which his death occurred, 1834, there was published in the *Star* an account of the organization of an anti-slavery society in Maine, and notice was given of a meeting to form such a society in New Hampshire. But in February, 1835, just one year after the publication of Bedee's article, there appeared, from the pen of Eld. Marks, a long article setting forth the character of slavery as it existed in the South, giving a summary of the laws relating to it, and depicting some of the horrors with which it was attended. The article closed with the following queries:

"1. Is not the state of things exhibited in the preceding the *natural result* which, in the present imperfect state of society, might be expected from the system of slavery?

"2. How can Christians, who are not blinded by self-interest, suppose such a system as slavery compatible with the infinite benevolence of the gospel?

"3. If the blacks have souls for whom Christ died, souls which must exist forever, can any *candid* man blame us for *writing, speaking, weeping* and *praying* on this subject, with the anxious hope that we may do something toward undoing a system of heavy burdens, and breaking the chains of the oppressed?"

This article was soon followed by other editorial articles, and by selections, taking the same view of the subject, and at length the paper had a department entitled, "Slavery." Although many of the subscribers, especially those in the South, were angry and ordered their papers discontinued, those having the immediate management of the paper were firm and decided in their course. They were soon strengthened in it by a resolution of the New Hampshire Yearly Meeting favoring it, and by the action of the General Conference, in 1835, which, though it said nothing respecting the position of the *Star*, pronounced against slavery, declared in favor of its abolition and recommended candid and mutual discussion as the best means of reaching this end. But there continued, both in and out of the denomination, a deep - seated opposition to the anti - slavery position of the *Star*, and there were those, ministers and laymen, who were untiring in their efforts to effect a change.

When the Trustees met in 1836, an act of incorporation had been refused by the Legislature of New Hampshire, the burden of debt was increasing, and many more were threatening to withdraw their patronage. The great question was,—" Shall *The Morning Star* pursue its present anti - slavery course?" Impressed with the importance of doing present duty and adhering to principle, the Board discussed the question with increasing earnestness, all day and into the night, and did not reach a decision until near the morning, when the vote was taken. Of the eleven present, all but one or two voted in the affirmative, and thus committed the *Star* in favor of liberty,—a decision never revoked, and momentous in its consequences. In this discussion Mr. Burr took a leading part, as he was the principal party arraigned; and such was the ability with which he sustained his position that some who had previously wavered were won to his views. All things considered, the triumph was one of the grandest sort, and marks one of the brightest spots in Mr. Burr's career.

But though defeated, the opposition was not subdued. To use Mr Burr's own language in speaking of this subject :

" This (last) contest continued in a most per-

sistent and virulent manner for many long years.
Ministers of our own denomination traversed New
Hampshire and Maine, denouncing the course of
the *Star*, and using their utmost efforts to destroy
its influence, and to create a public opinion in the
denomination which would either demand the removal of its conductors, or compel them to exclude the discussion of the subject of slavery from
its columns; while the papers of the pro - slavery
parties opened their batteries upon it, to counter-
act its damaging effects upon their corrupt political plans and prospects. But, thank God, victory came at last to the cause of liberty and justice."

But in spite of opposition, the paper gained in
strength and influence. It was largely owing to
its work that, in 1846, New Hampshire was lost to
the pro - slavery party, John P. Hale elected to
the United States Senate, and, among other
things, the Printing Establishment incorporated.
During the years which followed, the paper did a
noble work in preparing its readers for the great
storm which burst upon the nation in 1861; and
during all the years of the war, its tones were
clear, its faith was unfaltering, and its influence
in behalf of " Liberty and Union" immense. It
was a proud day for the Editor, when, at the
General Conference in 1865, and, as it proved,

almost at the completion of his grand career, he was able to say in his official report :

" Since the last Conference the *Star* has had the unspeakable joy of announcing the most important event of the nineteenth century, viz. : the overthrow and, as we hope in God, the final death of American slavery, for which it has so long and so arduously labored, and ardently hoped and prayed, but which· at times it has almost despaired of living to see. It is the Lord's doings, and marvelous in our eyes. To his great name be all the glory given."

One of the chief things which distinguished the anti - slavery position of the *Star* while under the editorial management of Mr. Burr, and for which it is deserving of great praise, was that it advocated the reform upon the basis of Christianity. While a class of laborers in the contest ignored the church, the *Star* sought to effect its purpose through the church. It ever regarded the spirit of Christianity and anti - slavery as in unison. The only difference that it knew between them was that the latter is the legitimate outgrowth of the former ; the one was the parent and the other the child; and when victory came, it felt that the triumph was, on this account, the more grand and complete.

———

It is difficult to estimate the influence and responsibility of an editor of a religious newspaper. He speaks to hundreds and thousands whom he has never seen, and of whom he may never have heard. While he is himself in the seclusion of his office, he is read by the wayside, in the place of business, and especially in the home circle where his name sometimes becomes a household word. His weekly offering affords mental and spiritual stimulus to all classes and conditions. It suggests thought to one, affords encouragement to another, and proves a warning to still another, and thus sets in operation a chain of influences the measure of which is infinite. Among the editors whose influence has been great, and whose sense of responsibility has been keen and constant, the name of BURR occupies a place second to but few.

IX.

THE TREASURER OF BENEVOLENT SOCIETIES.

The printing press has always been the friend and promoter of progress. Its invention served to arouse Europe from the slumbers of centuries, to give new impulse to learning of every kind and to prepare the way for the Reformation. The legitimate results of its work are still of a similar character.

From some points of view, the founding of *The Morning Star* at Limerick was a thing of no special significance. The time, however, when it was done and the peculiar circumstances attending it, served to render it an event important in its consequences. The denomination, in the interest of which it was published, was young and plastic. Imperfect in its organization, without general and systematized methods of operation and any special bond of union, it had nevertheless zeal and activity sufficient, if properly directed, to ac-

complish a grand work.   Indeed, it needed just
such an instrumentality as the *Star* proved, to
serve as a medium for the interchange of thought,
to suggest new plans of Christian effort and ways
and means for their prosecution, and to inspire the
body with high aims and noble purposes.

It is a significant fact that all the other great
enterprises of the denomination date their origin
subsequent to that of the *Star*, and it can be easily
shown that they are in an important sense indebted to it for their existence.   Of these other
enterprises, the Foreign Mission enterprise is the
oldest, the idea of which was first suggested by
the General Baptists of England.   In 1824, Rev.
James Peggs, a General Baptist missionary, then
in Cuttack, Orissa, addressed a letter " To the
churches and ministers of the Freewill Baptists in
America," in which he described the condition of
the heathen among whom he labored and asked
for co - operation.   This letter was published in
the *Star* in 1827, where it was read by hundreds,
and its contents pondered.   In 1832, the *Star*
contained a letter from Rev. Amos Sutton, then
a missionary in Orissa, in which he sought to en-

list the denomination in the foreign mission work.
The seed sown soon produced fruit, for early the
next year, 1833, the Foreign Mission Society was
organized with John Buzzell, then Senior Editor
of the *Star*, as President, and William Burr as
one of the Executive Committee. Had it not
been for the *Star*, through the columns of which
attention was called to the subject, if the Society
had existed at all, it would probably have dated
the commencement of its existence some years
later.

The connection between the *Star* and the origin of the Home Mission Society is still more direct. Says the compiler of " Marks's Life":—
" For several months, Mr. Marks had had his
sympathies greatly pained by his inability to answer favorably the numerous requests from different sections for laborers, addressed to him as
Agent of the Printing Establishment. These
calls continued to grow more numerous and importunate. In the early part of July, while he
and Mr. Burr were conversing upon this subject,
it was agreed that Mr. Marks should write a notice in the *Star*, calling a meeting for the forma-

tion of a Home Mission Society, to be held at
Dover, N. H., on Thursday, July 31, 1834, at
10 o'clock, A. M. Among other things append-
ed to the notice was the following,—'Some of
our brethren, when asked what they will do for
the Orissa Mission, have plead that they thought
there was need of doing something at home first.
. . . . Such brethren will now have an opportunity to show their faith by their works.' "
The Society was duly organized, and Eld. Marks
was chosen Corresponding Secretary and Mr.
Burr, Treasurer.

The *Star* early commenced to advocate the
cause of Sabbath schools. One of the results of
this advocacy was that the General Conference
directed the Publishing Committee, and afterwards the Trustees, to organize into a Sabbath
School Union, inviting others to membership
with them. Of this Union, Mr. Burr was the
Treasurer from the first. The anti-slavery sentiment of the denomination, fostered by the *Star*,
gave rise, in due time, to the Anti-Slavery Society. It would also be easy to show how the
influence of the *Star* contributed to found Par-

sonsfield Seminary and Strafford Academy, the oldest denominational schools, and to organize the Education Society.

To the origin of all these interests the *Star* not only contributed, but it has ever been to them a most powerful ally. It has defended the cause of each against opposition, spoken to them words of encouragement in despondency, and rejoiced with them in their prosperity. It would have been quite as natural for a mother to forsake her children, as for the *Star* to abandon the advocacy of these causes. And a reason for this is found in the fact that from the very first they had no truer friend and warmer supporter than the Editor of the *Star* and the Agent of the Printing Establishment.

Mr. Burr took an active part in the organization of the Foreign Mission Society, though he was not chosen Treasurer until 1837. Of the other Societies, he was not only present and assisted in their formation, but was also chosen Treasurer of them at the same time. Of all the Societies he continued Treasurer until 1864, when, in consequence of a conviction that the time had come for him to be relieved of a part of his responsibilities, he resigned the treasurership of the Education Society. Two years later as the result of an increased conviction of the same kind, he also resigned the same office in the Home Mission Society. Of the other Societies he continued to be Treasurer until his death. He was also a member of the Executive Committee of the Foreign Mission Society from its organization until his death, a member of the Executive Committee of the Home Mission Society almost from its formation until 1861, when he resigned and recommended another in his place; and he was for several years a member of the Executive Committtee of the Education Society.

During all the years which Mr. Burr acted as Treasurer of these Societies, notwithstanding the numerous additional burdens imposed upon him and the anxieties thereby caused him, he made no charge for his services. All that he did, he did as unto the Lord; and, at the same time, he contributed as much as any one of his means, for missions and education. When he resigned the Treasurership of the Education Society, it was voted to give him three hundred dollars as a slight compensation for the service rendered. But instead of receiving it for his own use, he gave it to found a four years' course of study for the benefit of such young men as could not devote a longer time,—a thing in which he felt a deep interest and earnestly advocated.

In the performance of his duties as Treasurer of the Benevolent Societies, together with those of a member of one, two or all, of the Executive Boards, he practiced the same economy, exercised the same forethought and manifested the same business qualities as in the management of the affairs of the Printing Establishment. He constantly felt that he was a keeper of the Lord's money, and that he was accountable to him as well as to men for the manner in which he fulfilled the responsible trust committed to him. Did either of the societies propose large outlays, he always had an eye to the financial side of the question. "Will the state of the treasury admit of it?" was a question which he repeatedly asked when new and, as he often regarded them, visionary schemes were proposed. From how many failures he, in this

way, saved the enterprises with which he was connected it is quite impossible to tell.

His judgment of men and measures was excellent. Nearly twenty years since, when the charge
of a St. Helena Mission was offered to the Foreign
Mission Board, he opposed its reception. Although members of the Board with whom he was
intimately associated and whom he dearly loved,
favored it, he could not. And when after pro-
tracted discussion, a vote to receive it was passed
by a small majority, he hoped that it would be re-
scinded, and labored for this object. The desired
result was soon realized, as subsequent develop-
ments unmistakably proved the correctness of
Mr. Burr's position. This is only one of the
many instances of the kind. It was his broad
views that especially qualified him to act as Treasurer of all the Benevolent Societies. He understood and felt the wants of each, and it is not
known that he was ever charged with partiality
for either. The fact that he continued Treasurer
and a member of the Executive Committee of the
Foreign Mission Society longer than of either of
the others Societies proves nothing. It was felt

that his counsels and labors in connection with this Society could not be spared. Money was often placed in his hands with the simple request that he would bestow it where it was most needed and would do the most good, and the injunction was always executed with the most conscientious fidelity. Although others sometimes differed from him, they were forced to give his opinions the deference to which years of experience in his special work entitled them. In periods of danger his counsel was most earnestly sought, and it was then that others most fully confided in him. The following letter, which is only one of the many of a similar character that might be reproduced, will tell its own story:

"BUFFALO, N. Y., March 17, 1862.
MY DEAR BRO. BURR:

I wish to breathe a few thoughts to you *privately* in regard to our Foreign Mission. Letters from India, for some months, have continued to give notice of Bro. Smith's failing health, yet I have all along hoped that he might be braced up during the present cold season so as to take a change to the mountains during the next hot season, and get on for a time without coming home. Your notice in the *Star* seems to be conclusive, and yet the fact that I have received

nothing which indicates positively that he was on
the point of leaving, leads me to hope a little, but
faintly.

But in case he is on his way home, what
next?

It will be two years or more, before Bro. Cooley can go back with renewed health. James
Phillips might be induced to go, though he would
much prefer to remain two or three years longer
so as to study medicine, nor would his going
materially help us in the present emergency.
We must pass two years, more critical than any
period of our mission, before either Bro. Cooley
or Bro. Smith can return. . . . . .

I have tried to look at this matter in all its
bearings, and weigh the chances for and against
us. With our present financial difficulties it
would be impossible to talk of *our* returning, nor
could *we* move with the necessary dispatch to
meet the difficulty. I have been thinking of this,
whether it would be judicious or possible for *me*
to step in to fill up this breach until Bro. Cooley
could return, leaving my family at home.

This is the only practicable plan I can devise
thus far. I drop these hints to you in confidence,
wishing them to go no further. Any plan that
would seem to you practicable, I have no doubt
the Executive Committee would coincide in.

Yours Truly,   O. R. BACHELER."

The last meeting of the Foreign Mission Board,
which Mr. Burr attended, was held at South
Berwick, but little more than a week previous to

his death. It was a meeting of much importance, and in some of its discussions which were more than usually animated, he took an active part and manifested some of his prominent characteristics.

The work performed by the several Benevolent Societies during the years in which Mr. Burr labored for them, stands in part as a monument to his memory. Its results may be seen in the Freewill Baptist churches in some of our cities and larger towns, which are now centers of influence; in the schools and colleges of the denomination, now among the most valuable and precious of its treasures; and in the Mission in India, which speaks in behalf of the faith and patience of the people which established it. Had not WILLIAM BURR lived, it is safe to presume that all these interests would have been far less numerous, strong and efficient. Many, not only in favored America, but also in distant heathen India, will rise up to call him blessed.

X.

THE DAILY LABORER.

Thus far, the reader has taken only a general and distant view of the subject of this biography. In this chapter, it is proposed to present him for close inspection and in the performance of his daily duties.

The subscriber who reads his paper,—*The Morning Star* for instance,—fresh from the office, little realizes the labor expended upon it, or considers through what processes it has passed before taking the form in which it is presented to his eye. A cursory glance, however, will teach him that its literary material may be divided into three parts, viz.,—such matter as is written by the editor or by editorial contributors, such as is furnished by ordinary contributors, and such as has been selected from other papers. From whatever source any of this material has come, it has cost the editor more or less labor. The editorial, written by the editor himself, is the result of patient and consecutive thought, and of the greatest care in composition. Conscious that he is writing for hundreds and thousands of critical readers, he is stimulated to give them his best ideas, expressed in the best possible manner. And from this work there is neither rest nor change. The lawyer is excessively busy only during the session of court, but the editor is always busy. The school-teacher has his regular vacations, but the editor's service is continuous. The minister who has been sick during the week, or engaged in duties outside of his calling, can exchange on the Sabbath, or use an old sermon; but the editor can resort to no such expedient. He must present fresh and vigorous thoughts upon the subjects which are agitating the public mind, and are calculated to interest the reader.

The editorials written by others must receive the editor's careful inspection, and he must decide whether the views expressed are such as he can endorse and are consistent with the unity of the paper. In this work he is required to discriminate closely and to judge correctly.

Many of the ordinary communications come into the hands of the editor in a very crude form; and, while many of them are rejected, others have to receive his careful revision. The selections, which seem to many to have cost the editor but little or no labor, are the result of much diligent research and careful discrimination. The short, pithy paragraph, which is read almost at a glance, may have required hours of patient toil to put it in its present form. The editor must watch closely public opinion, and be thoroughly conversant with the news of the day, so that he may present to his readers all the recent and important items of intelligence. It will not do for him to be found off his guard here. The offense is accounted almost unpardonable.

The material thus prepared must be in due proportion, so that the variety and form of the paper may be preserved, and must be dealt out to the compositors when they call for it. As respects this, the editor is usually the servant, and the compositors are the lords. They require not only to be served, but to be served immediately. The copy must also be distributed to them in such a way that each may have his due proportion of " fat" and "lean", or good copy and poor, or there will be chafing and discontent.

Constantly watching the progress of the work in the composing room, lest there may be an excess or deficiency of copy, the editor, at the proper time, directs his foreman how to arrange the articles, and the proof is soon taken, usually on sheets containing two columns each, and brought to him. This he examines with the utmost care, and marks each error with its appropriate sign. In this work a large number of faculties are called into exercise. The eye must see every letter and point, the orthography and punctuation must be corrected, and sometimes more suitable words chosen. The attention must be closely confined, for the least mental wandering or abstraction may result in a failure to detect an error which would seriously injure his reputation for correctness. After the editor has read the sheet, it is passed with the copy to proof-readers, one of whom reads the copy and the other looks upon the sheet, to see whether the latter agrees with the former, and mark such omissions as may be discovered, and typographical errors which, notwithstanding the careful reading it has received, may have been overlooked. The proof-sheet is then returned to the compositor to correct the errors discovered,—a work in which he takes no special delight. This being done, a revised proof is taken, which, with the original proof, is passed to the editor who compares the two, to learn if the compositor has faithfully performed his work. Such errors as have not been corrected are marked, the whole proof is again re-read, and the revised sheet is given to the compositor for further correction. A second revised proof is taken, when needful which is either examined by the editor, or by an experienced proof-reader. After the entire paper has been subjected to this process, it is adjudged ready for the eye of the public. The form is then laid down and given into the hands of the pressman. In the meantime, the editor is at work preparing material for another issue; and such is his routine of duties, week after week, and year after year. Mr. Burr performed this kind of work, as an Editor, for nearly forty years, in addition to his duties as a Publisher, and Treas-

urer of the Freewill Baptist Benevolent Societies.

After having thus described the process of
newspaper making, the writer would ask the
reader to spend a week with him in the office of
The Morning Star, in May, 1864. It is Monday morning, and the press - room is the center of
attraction. The Adams press is throwing off the
Star, at the rate of nearly a thousand copies per
hour. From the press the papers are run through
the folder quite as rapidly,—a process of much
interest to strangers. The papers are then
mailed by the use of Dick's mailing machine,
and sent to the Post Office. In the composing
room, the compositors are busy in marking and
measuring their work of the previous week;
but this is soon done, and then they commence
putting in type the matter for the outside of the
next week's paper. But to the Editor and Publisher, after inspecting the work in progress and opening the mail, this is a sort of holiday.

On Tuesday the solid work of the week, with
Mr. Burr, actually commences. The first thing
required of him—and this is true of each succeed-

ing morning of the week—is to satisfy himself that each person connected with the office is on duty, and that everything is in running order. Two hours are now devoted to business of various kinds. There are accounts to be adjusted, letters to be written before the close of the morning mail, the requisitions of various parties in and out of the office to be met, and various other things to be attended to, all of which make these two of the busiest hours of the day. At a little past ten, the carrier has brought the morning *Journal*, and everything else is laid aside for this; because it is war-time and the nation is in peril. Its contents are soon devoured, and every item of special interest is marked. When this is done, he goes for the morning mail, returning usually with from ten to fifty letters from all parts of the country, and with half this number of exchanges. The letters now receive his special attention. In the first place, each of them is opened with a paper-cutter and laid on the desk. He then takes each out of its envelope and reads it almost at a glance. The first, perhaps, contains a communication for the *Star*, and sometimes with the direction that it shall be "put in a conspicuous place and leaded." This is laid in its appropriate place. The second contains money, and he learns that a part of it is to pay for the *Star*, a part to pay for books, and the remainder is to be divided between one or both of the Mission Societies and the Education Society. He counts the money and writes the sum at the top of the letter, together with his initials, "W. B." A third letter contains both manuscript and money. The former is placed with the manuscript embraced in the first letter, and the letter is disposed of in the same way as the money contained in the second; and so with them all. When the letters are all thus treated, those which contained money are passed to the clerk, who examines them and credits the money on its appropriate book. The money brought by the morning's mail is deposited for safe keeping, and the work of the forenoon is usually completed.

The afternoon is devoted to such business suggested by the mail of the morning as demands immediate attention, in correcting communications, the preparation of editorial articles for the inside of the paper, and in general and miscellaneous work. In the evening he returns to the office and opens the evening mail, which is usually much smaller than that of the morning. This being done, he closes his office, for the reason that this is the night of the weekly prayer - meeting of the church, and he must attend it. On Wednesday all his time, except what is occupied by the imperative demands of business, is devoted to the reading of the outside of the paper, and this work sometimes occupies a portion of the evening. On Thursday he goes through very much the same routine of duties as on Tuesday, but perhaps more of his time is given to the preparation of copy. The evening, however, is spent in the office in the critical examination of exchanges. Friday morning is passed in very much the same manner as Tuesday and Thursday mornings. The afternoon and evening are occupied largely with the reading of the proof of the inside of the paper, and with the numerous little things requiring the personal attention of an editor. At the busiest moment, he is liable to be called upon by a compositor to decipher copy or to answer some question.

All things considered, this is to Mr. Burr the busiest and most trying day of the week. Saturday is spent largely in the completion of the work begun on Friday, and in the selection and preparation of copy for the outside of another issue ; and at night this copy is distributed among the compositors. During Friday and Saturday the outside of the paper has been printed, and to - night the inside is ready to go to press on Monday morning. Such are the ordinary labors of Mr. Burr for a single week.

During the week in May, the reader found Mr. Burr doing his regular work, but if he will spend a week with him during the earlier part of September, when the business of the Printing Establishment for the year is being closed up, he will find him doing extraordinary work.

No small item in Mr. Burr's daily labor was his correspondence. There were numerous questions to be answered, false impressions to be removed, solicited advice to be given, and various interests demanding attention. Of all letters relating to things of vital importance, or to subjects respecting which there was liable to be controversy, he retained copies. These copies, and the replies to their originals, or the letters to which their originals were replies, were carefully preserved for future reference. From the large amount of this correspondence still preserved, many interesting facts might be obtained and many secret things brought to light. But there are obvious reasons why this correspondence should remain, for the most part, undisturbed.

With the exception of reading proof, Mr. Burr usually performed his labor standing. This was, it is believed, owing to the fact that he regarded this posture more conducive to health than sitting. Many of the readers of this volume will remember how he appeared when at his standing desk in the old editor's room of the *Star* office.

With his habits of industry and application, one can readily conceive the immense amount of work which he must have performed during his life-time, first as printer, and afterwards as editor and publisher. He strictly obeyed the injunction, "Not slothful in business," and the daily laborer in any occupation can find in him an example eminently worthy of imitation.

The weekly routine of labor in the *Star* office is substantially the same now as it was during the life-time of Mr. Burr, though a much larger proportion of the copy is now prepared at the office, and the publication of books has brought a new and important element into the editor's sphere of service. The duties of editor and publisher are, however, now performed by two persons instead of by one, and the paper is half a day later in going to press. This last change was made at the time of the enlargement of the *Star* in 1868, so that the news of Monday morning might be inserted in the issue that goes to press in the afternoon.

XI.

Turning from the consideration of the more public acts of Mr. Burr, as they pertained to the denomination of his choice, the reader is now invited to take a view of him in other and, in some respects, more private relations. There were indeed many sides to his character, on neither of which does he seem to have been deficient. While his manhood was of the highest type, but few have ever performed more faithfully the duties of a Christian, a citizen, or those of a husband and father. His very presence revealed such a depth and fullness of meaning that no one could be mistaken respecting him.

The story of Mr. Burr's church relations is quickly told. As already stated, he was converted in 1828, and united with the Freewill

Baptist church in Limerick. On coming to Dover, in 1833, he united with the First Freewill Baptist church in this place. In February, 1840, he and twelve others were organized into what is now known as the Washington St. Church. He was then chosen one of its deacons, and he continued to serve in this relation until his death. Twice, in 1839 and 1862, he was chosen delegate to the General Conference of the denomination, and, on the former occasion, he acted as Secretary *pro tem.* of that body; though as a representative of the Printing Establishment, he attended every session of the Conference subsequent to 1830. For a year or two, 1839 and '40, he held a license to preach, but having become convinced that duty did not require him to exercise the functions of the sacred office, the idea of preaching was abandoned.

The conversion of Mr. Burr, an account of which has been given in a former chapter, was of the most thorough and radical character. Rarely has a work of grace been more complete. From the state of self - righteousness and self - sufficiency in which he had dwelt with a feeling of great

security, he came to see his own poverty and help-
lessness and the necessity of fleeing to Christ as
his only hope of salvation. He sought constantly
to maintain a vital union with Christ. He was,
especially during his earlier Christian experience,
sensitive to the least fluctuations in his religious
enjoyment. He rejoiced, or was depressed, just
in proportion as he believed his heavenly Father
smiled or frowned upon him. He entered the
service of the great Master as a laborer. As
already seen, he had scarcely indulged a hope
before he urged his apprentice to seek Jesus with
him. From the first, he was a constant attendant
upon all the means of grace, especially the prayer-
meeting. Sometimes he would go miles to attend
one, and his voice was invariably heard in prayer
and exhortation. One of the most transparent of
men, a conscientious fidelity was apparent in all
his acts. The few pages already given from his
journal contain a vivid portraiture of his early
Christian experience. To many it is believed that
no pages in this little volume will be more re-
plete with interest. The experience of later
years was the legitimate out-growth of that of

those early years. If the former was the small and bubbling rill, the latter was the broad, deep river.

He ever sought to maintain a firm adherence to the right, and his standard of rectitude was at the same time exalted. The idea of doing things, or failing to do them, from motives of expediency, seems to have formed no part of his mental constitution. Whatever others might do, he could never countenance a wrong act anywhere, much less in the church. Although his views in regard to this subject might involve him in difficulty, yet he could not swerve from his conscientious convictions of duty. Such a course he believed that God would neither bless nor the world approve.

He could never knowingly do a wrong act, and whenever he discovered that he had inadvertently done so, he could have no enjoyment until the injury was repaired. He felt that before he could be at peace with God, his Father, he must have a reconciliation with man, his brother.

He maintained a constancy and faithfulness in the performance of what he regarded as his whole duty. He was never what is termed a backslider. Though his experience was more or less varied, he never turned aside from the path which he had chosen, from the day of his conversion to that of his death. He was ever constant and faithful in the performance of his religious duties in the family and the prayer - meeting. He was absent from the latter only in case of absolute necessity, and when present he almost invariably occupied the same seat. No one usually enjoyed the meeting more than he, and he sometimes drank in of its spirit to overflowing. In prayer he was satisfied only when he felt that he was talking with the Eternal as in his very presence chamber. In exhortation, though he was sometimes slow of utterance, there was a power in his words that the most thoughtless could not but feel. He was constantly troubled, lest he should fail to do his whole duty. In the "Scraps from his Journal," the reader has seen how he felt in regard to his conduct toward his brother Elijah while on a visit with him, and this feeling seems to have been characteristic. It led him at one time to raise the question whether he ought not to enter the ministry, and it was some time before he could be persuaded that he was preaching to a larger audience from his place in the *Star* office than the occupant of any pulpit in America. His allegiance to his heavenly Father was complete, and he felt that his claims upon him were imperative.

But his sense of obligation did not terminate here. He felt that others had claims upon him. This led him to contribute liberally for the support of the ministry and the various benevolent enterprises of the day. Yet his religion did not consist entirely in giving, but in *doing*, as well. The many acts of kindness which he did and the repeated words of encouragement which he spoke, all told of his goodness of heart and the noble aims of his life,—things which arrested attention and commanded respect.

It is not known that, during all his years of Christian experience, any one ever doubted his piety, unless he sometimes doubted it himself. Even those who had no respect for religion, could say nothing against his manner of life, while, on the other hand, it was to them a perpetual warning. Since his death, an impenitent woman has been heard to say that she had been to

his door to listen to him while engaged in
family devotions. On the day of his funeral, no one seemed to be a more sincere mourner
than a woman of another faith and another nationality who had served in his family.
She came to his residence to take a last look of
his lifeless remains and went with the procession
as it moved to the church, manifesting at the
same time great sorrow. Such incidents tell
their own story.

Thus was Mr. Burr an embodiment of some of
the rarest and best Christian virtues; and manifesting these through a period of nearly forty
years of Christian walk, his daily life told largely
for the honor of God and the good of his fellow
men. Rarely has there been a better specimen,
among the laity, of the type of Christianity developed by the denomination with which he was connected. As was said of him in an editorial in the
Star, the week following his death,—" Religion
was the governing principle of his life, and, as
such, regulated all his acts."

After the organization of the Washington Street
church, in 1840, this was emphatically Mr. Burr's

spiritual home. Chiefly instrumental in its formation, he gave it all the strength and influence he could exert, though he never manifested a narrow sectarian spirit. The band of brethren and sisters that composed the church was at first small and weak, but it gradually increased in numbers and strength. From the small room over one of the stores on Central Street, where the church was organized, they soon removed to the "Old Court House," in which they worshiped until the completion of the Old Church on Washington Street, in 1843. Under the labors of the first three pastors, Davis, Moulton and Dunn, each of whom served but a short term, the foundations of a permanent interest were laid, while under the long pastorate of the lamented Hutchins, which commenced in 1845 and continued thirteen years, the church became a power for good scarcely second to any church in the place. In the accomplishment of this result, the influence and labors of Mr. Burr, from some points of view, were at each period quite as important as those of the pastor. He early made upon the church his own impress, and sought to mold it in accordance with his ideas of what a church should be. From the first it took an advanced position upon all the reforms of the day, such as missions, temperance, anti-slavery and the like, and its membership was composed largely of earnest Christian workers.

During all these years, the interests of the church lay very near his heart. No one thanked the Lord more heartily when it prospered, or grieved more sorely in its adversity. From the first the growth of the church was almost without interruption, and but few have been the instances in which an enterprise of the kind has been conducted with greater union of feeling. The acknowledged leader in both the temporal and spiritual affairs of the church, no one of all the numerous and valuable co-laborers who came to his assistance, seems to have been jealous of his position or influence. The great secret of his success in this particular consisted in the fact that, while he was disposed to consult the wishes and feelings of all as far as practicable, it was very apparent that, in all his acts, self-interest was subordinate to the good of the cause. And sometimes when there might have been a division of feeling arising from a partial view of the case in hand, when all the facts came to be known, every breath of discontent was hushed.

It is quite unnecessary to say more respecting Mr. Burr's character and labors as a Christian. There are hundreds, if not thousands, of living witnesses who can testify of these things, and upon whom his example has left its impress. The Washington Street church, so largely the result of his labors, will continue to speak in his praise, and eternity alone will fully reveal what was accomplished by his life. The memory of such a man and Christian is blessed.

It is common to speak of churches as the result of the labors and sacrifices of ministers. Is it not, however, often the case that the instrumentality of pious and influential laymen is quite as important? To be the means, under God, of founding a church that will continue for generations to exert a saving influence in a community, is something worthy of a life-time of toil in the service of the Master. Let none be weary in well-doing.

XII.

THE CITIZEN AND PHILANTHROPIST.

In such a man as Mr. Burr it is difficult to distinguish between his character as a Christian and his character as a citizen. What he was as the latter, as well as in all the other relations of life, was largely the outgrowth of what he was as the former.

Mr. Burr held no office strictly political until six or seven years previous to his death, when he occupied, for two or three years, a prominent place in the City Government, and was for two years a member of the Legislature. But this fact indicates but little respecting the nature of his work and influence. Restrained from seeking office by his characteristic modesty, and the fact that the party to which he belonged was for many years in the minority, his numerous duties did not allow him to hold it. Nevertheless his influence was constantly felt in favor of the right and in opposition to the wrong.

The thirty-three years during which Mr. Burr was a citizen of Dover, embraced almost the entire period of the great anti-slavery conflict, and through all these years, he was an anti-slavery man in the capacity of a citizen as well as that of an editor. An opponent of Jackson's administration, he was for some years identified with the Whig party, and he not only believed in the general soundness of its policy, but he also respected its intelligence. Feeling, however, that the party as a whole was not committed in opposition to slavery, he separated himself from it. As early as 1840 or '41, he and a few others voted what was known as the "Liberty Ticket," and thus commenced in Dover a political party which continued its existence until 1855, when there was a recast of parties, and the principles for which the anti-slavery party had contended were embodied in those of the party dominant in the city and in the state. The third party, of which Mr. Burr was a leader, was always small, yet it was this same small band of reformers, composed of earnest, thoughtful and true-hearted men, that received Hon. John P. Hale with open arms, when he was cast out of the pro - slavery party in 1845. Contending constantly and steadily for a great idea, they went bravely forward to the accomplishment of a noble work, and were eventually rewarded with a triumph most grand and complete. Viewing things from our stand - point, we can not but honor, nay, reverence, the noble pioneers in the anti - slavery reform, who were willing to struggle on year after year, "steady through evil report and good report, through honor and dishonor," that they might maintain a great principle and become the benefactors of an oppressed race.

Mr. Burr was, during those years, what might be termed a practical anti - slavery man. More than once the hunted fugitive found protection within his dwelling, and was speeded by him in his flight from bondage to liberty. A story is told of him that on one occasion his earnestness of manner was so misunderstood that it came near having an effect opposite to the one intended. One morning as he was deeply engaged in business, a fugitive, who had grown gray in the service of a southern master, entered his office and gave him a letter of introduction from a Friend residing in Philadelphia. As the colored man passed the letter to him, he tremblingly inquired, "Are you an abolitionist?" Mr. Burr, reading the letter, at once replied, "I am abolitionist enough to take care of you." The emphasis and almost sternness with which these words were uttered, terrified the poor fellow, who feared that he had fallen into the hands of an enemy. The kindness, however, with which he was treated, and the hospitable manner in which he was received into Mr. Burr's home, soon quieted all his fears, and he came to feel and know that he had found a friend indeed.

While Mr. Burr belonged to the party in the minority, his labors in behalf of the cause of liberty were untiring. His presence and words cheered his few associates even in the darkest hour. But when he became a member of the party in the majority, his efforts did not cease, though somewhat changed in their direction. He was especially solicitous that the party be kept pure, and that none but good men be selected for office. Consequently, he made it a special point to attend the primary meetings of the party. Sometimes, when not more than a dozen were present at one of these meetings, he was one of the number. In this way he accomplished more for the principles which he advocated than a large number of well - meaning men who think it unnecessary to attend a political caucus, and thereby forget that, for the stream to run clear, the fountain must be kept pure.

During the war of the rebellion, no man felt more deeply for his country's welfare, or prayed more earnestly for its salvation. His spirits were elevated or depressed just in proportion as the army of liberty met with successes or reverses, yet his faith in ultimate victory was ever firm. On Monday morning, when the fall of Richmond was announced, his heart overflowed with thankfulness to the Giver of victory. Returning to the office from "the bulletin board," where he was usually one of the first to learn the news, he hastily prepared a brief statement of the great event for insertion in the paper, which was then being issued. As he gave it to the compositor, calling her by name, he said,—"You never put in type a paragraph containing news of such a glorious character." But the heart then exultant was, in less than two weeks later, pierced with deep sorrow, as were the hearts of thousands all over our land, at the death of our martyred Lincoln. In the suppression of the rebellion and the consequent overthrow of slavery, he felt that the labors, prayers and sacrifices of a life-time in the cause of liberty had been more than abundantly rewarded, and fittingly might he thus feel, since the Master's approval was, "Because thou hast labored and not fainted."

The writer is pleased to receive the following testimony, respecting the character of Mr. Burr as an anti-slavery man, from a source which renders it especially valuable:

"DOVER, N. H., Oct. 10, 1870.
MY DEAR SIR:
You asked me for some brief statements of my recollections of Mr. Burr, especially of his character as an anti-slavery man, and his fidelity to principle.

When I first knew Mr. Burr, I knew him simply as a quiet, unobtrusive editor of a weekly religious newspaper printed in Dover, called, *The Morning Star*, steadily and unostentatiously devoting himself to the multifarious duties of his profession.

When the anti-slavery controversy first manifested itself in New England, it found arrayed against it the organized religious and political action of a vast majority of the members of all denominations. But Mr. Burr viewed the question from a different stand-point than those by whom he was surrounded. It presented itself to his mind simply as a question of duty. Having clear convictions on the subject himself, the course he was to pursue appeared to him a plain one,— to follow those convictions to their legitimate result, entirely irrespective of any consequences which might affect him or his interests in any point of view.

It required no ordinary nerve in a young man at that time, thus to separate himself from the opinion of those about him. Almost solitary and alone he devoted himself and the press with which he was connected to the great cause of suffering and down-trodden humanity; satisfied that he was *right*, he did not stop to inquire if his course was popular. From this time Mr. Burr was open and decided upon this question, as he always was upon all subjects to which he gave his attention. His was no timid, cautious, calculating support, but an entire surrender of himself and all his interests to the advocacy of human rights.

He was an early, steadfast, heroic advocate and protector of the hunted fugitive, even in those days when it was dangerous to harbor a runaway slave; no fugitive was ever

turned away from his door without having received
the sympathy and aid which his case demanded.
It is indeed difficult in these days to realize the
obloquy and danger attending protection thus afforded.

Mr. Burr lived to see the triumph of the great
principles which he had advocated, lived to see
them the controlling policy of the country, yet,
although a pioneer in the cause now become
popular, he asked no office or favor from the
Government. His life flowed on tranquilly in
our midst, and when death snatched him away,
the prayers of the ransomed ascended to Heaven
for him, and a glorious company welcomed him to
the eternal city.   JOHN P. HALE."

As already stated, Mr. Burr held no office
strictly political until six or seven years previous
to his death. He was then, for two years, a
member of the City Government, and his weight
of character, together with his business qualities,
pointed to him as the member most suitable to
preside over the branch to which he belonged.
For two years later, 1862 and '63, he was elected
to the Legislature. In consequence of the war,
this was a critical period, and the exercise of much
wisdom and judgment was required of a legislator.
Though making but few speeches and not always
voting with his party, in the language of one of

his associates, "Mr. Burr's words, whenever he did speak, carried weight, and he was soon regarded as one of the most reliable and influential members of the House." Among his more important and praiseworthy acts, while a member of the Legislature, were his efforts in behalf of Gov. Berry. The duties and responsibilities of the Governor were largely increased in consequence of the war, and it was simply an act of justice that he should receive some additional compensation. The politicians with whom he was not particularly popular sought to deprive him of this, but Mr. Burr, always a friend of justice, interested himself in his behalf and gained the end sought. In response to a note from the writer, Gov. Berry recognizes the service rendered, and pays a beautiful tribute to Mr. Burr's memory. His letter is as follows :

"ANDOVER, MASS., Sept. 24, 1870.
REV. J. M. BREWSTER :

DEAR SIR, — Yours of the 22d inst. is before me, and in answer to your inquiries I would say, that I have a very distinct and pleasing recollection of Mr. Burr. From the short personal acquaintance I had with him, and from what I had learned of him otherwise, I truly

considered him one of the best of men, and when
I heard of his death, I felt sad that so good a man
had been taken from us. I distinctly recollect
that he ever manifested a deep interest in my
behalf while I occupied (at that time) the very
responsible position of Governor of New Hampshire. He thought that I was justly entitled to
compensation in addition to what had been the
usual salary of the Governor of the State, in as-
much as my duties and responsibilities were far
greater than those of any Governor before me,
and he therefore used his influence with other
representatives in my behalf. I shall ever remember Mr. Burr with affectionate gratitude, not
only for the part he took in relation to my salary,
but also for the deep sympathy and Christian
counsel and advice I received from him, when I
felt the need of these things as I never felt them
before.   Very Truly Yours,

N. S. BERRY."

To the necessities of the poor Mr. Burr's heart
was always open, and his hand ready to relieve
when he was convinced of their wants. With other
citizens of Dover, he waged war with intemper-
ance at an early day, when legal as well as moral
suasion was used. He contributed his share in
securing for the city its present and excellent
system of public schools, and, in a word, he was
always among the foremost in every good work,

and his name was a terror to evil doers. Such were his character and reputation, that no one was in doubt respecting the side of any moral question on which he was to be found. For several years he was a member of the Board of Directors of Strafford bank, and his financial ability rendered him one of its most efficient members. Dover has lost few of its citizens whose death brought a larger calamity or suggested stronger reasons for lamentation.

XIII.

It is scarcely necessary to say that Mr. Burr was, during all the years of his married life, a devoted husband. Indeed, he was in this relation all that might have been expected of a man who acted so well his part in so many other relations in life.

To these parents were born nine children, — six sons and three daughters, — only three of whom, two sons and one daughter, survive their father. These facts at once suggest an intermingling of joy and sorrow in these parents' hearts, a succession of sunshine and shadow along their pathway.

The first death in their household was that of little Harriet Ann, in the early spring of 1838. During the month of April, 1850, Death twice came and took away two boys, Charles Henry and James Albert, aged respectively seven and five.

Thus early in their experience of sorrow, though their hearts had been thrice torn, these grief-stricken parents came to feel,

"That most our Heavenly Father cares
For whom he smites, not whom he spares,"

and, clinging closer to his side, they bowed their heads and kissed the rod.

But other and more unwelcome lessons were to be taught them in the school of affliction.

Of all the children, no one seems to have been so much the pride of his father as the eldest, William Waters. In the twenty-fifth year of his age, of a generous nature, ambitious of honor obtained only by devotion to duty, well educated and possessed of strong mental powers,

"Seldom, in youth, is brighter promise given
Of a rich noon, or more effulgent day."

For some years he had been connected with the Treasury Department at Washington, and after a short vacation spent at home, with failing health, he returned to Washington in December, 1856, as it proved, to die. Prompt to duty, he immediately wrote to his father, under date of December 15, as follows :

" My Dear Father :

　　　　　Here I am at my desk, and the

first thing will be to finish this letter. . . . .
I unpacked the medicine and found all safe, and
now I am, as already stated, at my desk. It is
somewhat warmer here than in Dover. As to
my health, I really do not know what to say. I
am not quite so hoarse, but how in the world I
got here, I am sure I can not explain. I have
seen some rough times. I have but time now to
close, for I was assured by Gov. Anderson this
morning that I had been missed exceedingly, and
that they hardly knew what they should do without me. I find my desk *heaped* with work.
Poor me! Love to all. Tell mother the medicine was all right.

Affectionately,   W. W. BURR."

This seems to have been the last letter which
he wrote to his father. He continued to decline
rapidly, yet with an indomitable will and a hero-
ism with which the invalid only is acquainted, he
sought his accustomed work almost until the summons came, which was on the evening of the 24th
of January, 1857. The father and mother had
previously left home for Washington, hastily
summoned thither by a telegram sent without the
knowledge of William, but not to reach the
city until after his death.

No event connected with his life seems to have

caused Mr. Burr so much anguish of soul as the death of this son. He grieved, and grieved sorely. Though sympathy was proffered on every hand, and though he felt that he had the prayers of thousands, yet relief was found only in looking to the Great Helper, and the promise became manifest, —" As thy day, so shall thy strength be."

Judged from a human stand-point, this affliction would have seemed sufficient to stamp upon him, " perfect through suffering," but God saw it otherwise, and he was to drink deeper of the bitter cup.

In March, 1860, a little more than three years after the death of William Waters, John M., the eldest surviving son, then in the twentieth year of his age, passed peacefully and triumphantly to the other shore; and in March, 1863, a little less than three years later still, they buried Emma, a beloved daughter, then in the vigor of early womanhood.

Thus we get some idea of the character of Mr. Burr's domestic sorrows during these years. But though overwhelming, they served to a nature like his, to deepen and elevate rather than conquer. Stricken, bereft, bright hopes withered, joys torn away, his confidence remained unshaken in the goodness of his heavenly Father. Amid all the darkness, his faith did not let go its hold on the eternal wisdom, and rest and refuge were found in the sympathy of Christ. With one of old he was able to rise up and say, " The Lord gave and the Lord hath taken away ; blessed be the name of the Lord !"

Mr. Burr's was eminently a Christian home. Religion was the golden thread which ran through all the web of his domestic life. On the day on which he was married an altar was set up, and incense was kept constantly burning thereon until the day of his death. To the children the best moral and Christian instruction was given. Whatever interest the father manifested in their education or solicitude for their worldly prosperity, he felt even greater interest and solicitude for their personal salvation. Frequent conversations were sought and each opportunity striven to be embraced to urge it upon their attention. His faith in the efficacy of prayer was strong. That which

helped him bear the death of his eldest son was
the fact, brought to his knowledge by a teacher of
William, that he daily found enjoyment in carrying his wants to his heavenly Father. Often-
times his prayers for the conversion of his children were very importunate, and these prayers
were offered to a covenant - keeping God. "The
promise is unto you and to your children."

————

The death of Mr. Burr left a sad vacancy in
all the positions which he so acceptably and hon-
orably filled. But there is no place from which
he is so much missed, or where his absence is so
deeply mourned, as in his own home to which
his presence was always a benediction. In this
home, from which so many loved ones have gone
to be tenants of heavenly mansions, there linger
blessed memories, and grateful hearts look up
through their tears and thank God for the influence of a holy life.

"Oh, though oft depressed and lonely,
    All my fears are laid aside,
If I but remember only
    Such as these have lived and died."

XIV.

While Mr. Burr's name was familiarly spoken in so many households, he was personally known to comparatively few. Confined to his office by his numerous duties, he traveled but little, and then, for the most part, to attend denominational gatherings. The engraved likeness at the commencement of this little volume, will, therefore, serve as a pleasant reminder to those who knew him personally, and it will be of scarcely less interest to the larger class who never looked upon his pleasant features and noble form. The likeness is from a photograph taken less than two years previous to his death, and presents him as he appeared in his later years, with his genial expression, free from a sense of care. When engaged in business or burdened with anxiety, he wore an expression somewhat stern.

In his tastes and habits, Mr. Burr was averse
to ostentation in dress and manners, but he was
in the highest sense of the word a gentleman.   In
early life he was frail in form and youthful in
appearance, so that at thirty - five years of age
he could have easily passed for twenty - five.   In
middle life, he suffered considerably from ill
health, resulting largely from close confinement
to his work.   Some ten years previous to his
death, much anxiety was manifested lest he should
break down under his burden of responsibility.
He rallied, however, and during the last six or
eight years, he became somewhat robust in form
and appearance.   This was owing largely to the
fact that he was more regular and systematic in
taking exercise.   He practiced horse - back rid-
ing much, and found it very beneficial.   In the
later hours in the afternoon, he could be almost
invariably seen on some of the pleasant drives
about Dover upon his pony, which he kept almost exclusively for this purpose.   These rides
served to him as agreeable pastimes, and doubtless aided in prolonging his life for years.   Sometimes he rode in his carriage and invited a friend

to accompany him.   At such times he was one of the most chatty and companionable of men, delighting to rehearse some early experience or to discuss interests pertaining to the passing moment.

In midsummer, he sometimes snatched a day or two from the hurry of business to visit Hingham, or to take a pleasure trip to the Isle of Shoals, or some other point.   On such days he usually forgot his business cares and devoted himself to recreation as far as it is possible for a man of his habits to do ; and, as the natural result, he returned refreshed and invigorated.

———

While, as just intimated, Mr. Burr made most of his longer journeys to attend denominational gatherings, this was not exclusively the case.   In the summer of 1838, he left the *Star* in charge of Rev. E. Mack, and went to what was then known as the " Far West," —a great undertaking for those times.   He traveled in company with Rev. Mr. Spaulding, of the M. E. church, and gave a graphic account of their experiences in a series of letters in the *Star*.   They left Boston, on the 22d of June, by rail for Stonington, where they took a steamer for New York. They enjoyed a pleasant sail up the Hudson to Albany, whence they went to Utica by rail. Taking a canal passage to Rochester, they again traveled by rail to Batavia. Thence going by stage to Buffalo, they there took a steamer for Detroit. Of this place he said:

"We arrived at Detroit on Saturday, June 30, at half-past six, A. M., just one-half hour too late to take the cars for Ypsilanti, and were therefore under the necessity of remaining in Detroit until Monday; for though the cars left on Sunday morning, we of course were not disposed to profane God's holy day. Detroit contains 8,200 inhabitants. Some of the buildings are well and handsomely built, but far the greater part are of an inferior character."

Near Kalamazoo they were obliged to purchase horses, and to make most of the journey west of this point on horseback. At a place which he calls " Little Prairie Ronde," they visited Rev. S. L. Julian, " the first convert" in the " Limerick revival," who accompanied them in their travels further west. Of Chicago, where they arrived on the 11th of July, he said:

"We are somewhat disappointed in this place. The buildings are too scattering to appear to advantage. Most of them are small and poorly built—but few blocks of handsome. buildings. The houses are scattered along the shore for three or four miles, and one or two miles inland. There can hardly be said to be a regularly built street in all the place, though it contains a population of 5,000. Its commercial advantages, however, will eventually render it a large city. It stands on the border of a low, flat prairie, which is, some part of the year, covered with water. In the vicinity nothing is to be seen but the lake on one side, and on the other, one vast plain with woods far away in the distance; on the north the woods appear nearer the city. Here is room to build a city as large as London."

During a portion of their journey their experiences were somewhat severe. In a new and sparsely settled country, they sometimes lost their way; and when night came, if they were fortunate enough to find a stopping-place, their accommodations were extremely poor, and their landlords were sometimes of a doubtful character. On one occasion, as Mr. Burr used to tell the story in later years, after having traveled nearly all day through the woods, at night they came to a small log cabin tenanted by a man and his wife

whose appearance was not at all prepossessing.
Learning that there was no other habitation for
miles distant, with considerable reluctance they
concluded to remain for the night.   Vacillating
between hope and fear, just as they retired to
their small and poorly furnished lodging - place,
they espied behind the door several copies of
The Morning Star suspended upon a wooden
hook.   For Mr. Burr this was sufficient.   He
felt safe in a house where the *Star* was taken ;
and dismissing all further anxiety, he enjoyed a
good night's rest.   Before leaving, he could
scarcely persuade his landlord that he was the
veritable Editor of the *Star*, as he seemed to be
possessed with the idea that the Editor of such a
paper must be something " more than an ordinary man."

Mr. Burr's description of a night spent between
Janesville and Mineral Point, Wisconsin, is particularly interesting.   It seems that, as there was
no habitation for thirty miles, the party expected
to encamp, and made some preparation accordingly.   They found themselves encamped at night in
the middle of an extensive high - rolling prairie at

the foot of an old and large oak tree, more or less wet by a shower of the afternoon. Here they built a fire and tried to make themselves as comfortable as possible. He says :

"In this situation, we remained until past twelve o'clock, the thunders rattling through the concave, and the lightnings flashing with great vividness from west to east and east to west, without scarcely a cessation during the whole time. The grandeur and sublimity of the scene which we witnessed during the night are seldom surpassed even in the works of nature. At one moment the heavens and the broad swells of the high prairie, which stretched out before us as far as the eye could reach, were splendidly lighted up by the vivid lightning's flash ; and the next, dense darkness surrounded us, and loud rumbling thunder seemed to shake the earth to its center. It was but a faint emblem, however, of that awful day 'when the heavens shall be rolled together as a scroll and the elements be melted with fervent heat.'"

Mr. Burr arrived at his home on the 25th of August, after an absence of nine weeks. During this time he traveled not less than three thousand miles, and visited nine states and one territory.

All things considered, this was the most note-worthy journey of Mr. Burr's life, though he made others quite as long. At the close of the General Conference held at Maineville, Ohio, in October, 1856, he and others crossed the Ohio River, penetrated Kentucky, went as far as Lexington and Ashland, and visited the homes of Henry Clay and John C. Breckenridge, the latter a candidate for the Vice - Presidency. On his return home, he and Rev. S. Curtis visited Washington, where his son William was then a clerk.

Many of the writer's personal recollections of Mr. Burr are particularly pleasing. Well does he remember the morning in March, 1864, when he entered the office of the *Star*, and asked Mr. Burr, who was standing at his desk, for his influence in securing a position which was then named. Removing his glasses, he promptly replied with one of his significant smiles, "I will do so if you desire it, but I have other work for you." As the result of this interview, the writer entered the office a few weeks later and became Mr. Burr's assistant. During the entire period he was with him, so uniformly kind was all his bearing, so vaulable were his counsels, and so unceasing was his interest, that he came to regard him as a father, and as such he cherishes his remembrance.

Recollections of Mr. Burr during the last year of his life are especially fresh. Through a large portion of the month of December, 1865, he was confined by sickness. For a few days his situation was considered critical. He was, however, soon able to attend to his usual routine of duties. For a few days in the earlier part of June, he was confined again, and was scarcely able to make the journey by his own private conveyance to be present at the New Hampshire Yearly Meeting held at Holderness — a gathering which he invariably attended, and in the proceedings of which he always took an active part. Many will call to mind his very appropriate remarks on taking the chair at this meeting, and the grace and dignity with which he filled it. In July he visited his native town for the last time, and in September attended the Vermont Yearly Meeting, and spent a few days with Rev. S. Curtis amid the delightful scenery of the Green Mountains, returning in season to be present at the meeting of the Corporators.   After attending the Anniversaries at Lawrence early in October, and the Foreign Mission meeting at South Berwick a week or two later, he was to be seen no more at the gatherings of the denomination, where his presence had been for years most warmly welcomed and his service highly valued ; — he had become one of the great assembly before the throne of God.

While Mr. Burr was not a singer, but few enjoyed good music better than he. The week previous to his death, a musical convention was held in Dover, at which several highly trained singers, including Mrs. D. C. Hall, of Boston, were present. The singing of this lady almost enraptured him ; — especially was this the case in her rendering of the piece, entitled, "Birdy Looking out for Me," a beautiful and touching poem, which this lady sang most skillfully and effectively. The next day he would not be satisfied until he had found the poetry,* read it to Mrs. Burr, who had not heard it sung, and laid it aside for publi-

*Published in the *Star* of Jan. 2, 1867.

cation in the *Star*. As it proved, his ear was being tuned for the richer and sweeter music of heaven.

Already had his spiritual life become quickened, his prayers more fervent and his mention of his future home more frequent. His work on earth was being finished, and the faithful servant was to be called to his rest and reward in his Father's house above. Indeed, the door stood wide open, and he was soon to enter.

XV.

In taking his servants to himself, God employs different methods. Sometimes he does it by means of a long and lingering sickness, and thus affords a warning of the approaching change. At other times, he summons them into his immediate presence without premonition. In such cases, though not translated as were Enoch and Elijah, yet, ripe for heaven, they are relieved at once from the labors and conflicts of earth, and the presence and glory of God, with all the heavenly hosts, are suddenly and unexpectedly revealed to their enraptured vision. As regards the manner of his death, Mr. Burr belongs to the last named class.

Sunday, Nov. 4, 1866, was a beautiful, late autumn day. The sun shone clear and bright, while scarcely a cloud was to be seen. The day was especially favorable to church-going, and almost everywhere the house of God was filled with devout worshipers. On this day, Mr. Burr occupied his accustomed seat in the Washington Street church. It being the first Sabbath in the month, at the close of the second service the Lord's Supper was observed. As deacon of the church, he occupied his place at the altar and passed the sacred emblems, prepared on this occasion with his own hands. Though the season was impressive and peculiarly precious, it was not expected that one of those present,—and especially he whom all loved and honored as a father and friend,—was, before the rising of another sun, to eat bread and drink wine in the kingdom of God.

On the previous evening, after spending an hour or two in the examination of exchanges, Mr. Burr had left the office and the very chair which he had occupied for twenty-three years. During the day, as observed by his family, he was unusually cheerful, and several who saw him at church remarked that he manifested more than his usual vigor and freshness. He spent much of the day while at home in conversation with his daughter and her husband, who were then returning from Buffalo to Bangor. At his family devotions that evening he read the hymn commencing,

" The leaves around me falling,
Are preaching of decay,"

remarking, at the same time, that it was a favorite hymn.

At the prayer-meeting in the evening, he was in his accustomed seat, and joined in the exercises, both by prayer and exhortation. In the former he was more than usually fervent. Referring to the future world, he said,—" We have friends there; some of them have passed the river only just before us." With the utterance of these words, his feelings overcame him and he paused, to recover himself in a few moments. In his exhortation, later in the meeting, he referred to the Christian warfare, to which the sermon of the afternoon had special reference, and urged upon Christians the importance of "fighting the good fight of faith." He also spoke of the shortness of time and the importance of improving it. Speaking of his own life, he said that it seemed to him he had accomplished but little, and he desired to renew his consecration, and thereby pledge himself to increased fidelity. In closing, he appealed to the large number of young men present to consecrate themselves to Christ, that they might become useful in his service and thus accomplish the great end of life. He believed that God designed some of them for the ministry. His remarks were a noble testimony for Jesus, and in every way worthy to be the dying words of such a man and Christian.

A few minutes before eight o'clock, he rose and attempted to remove his overcoat, but sank back upon his seat. Some who had observed that his movements were not entirely natural, went to him and learned that he was sick and wished to retire. It was soon discovered that he had been seized with what might prove to be apoplexy, yet all hoped that the stroke might not be fatal. He was soon carried by his brethren from the church to his grief-stricken family. He spoke but few words after he was seized, and these with difficulty. On his arrival home he seemed to recognize his wife and daughter, but soon became unconscious. Every means in human power was used for his relief, but to no purpose. He grew worse, and about two o'clock in the morning it became evident that his end was near.

During the hour following, there stood around him his devoted family and a few long - tried but now weeping friends. Angels hovered over that dying scene, and all could not but rejoice in view of the prospects which awaited him who was about to depart to his eternal home. At three o'clock, his convulsions ceased, and it became apparent that his time had fully come. He breathed easily once or twice, and then his spirit took its departure. The gates of heaven opened widely for its entrance, and there was joy at its advent. Three hours later, the *Star* announced to the community, the denomination and the world that its honored Editor and Publisher was no more.

On the following Wednesday, he was buried from the Washington Street church. An appropriate funeral discourse was preached by Rev. S. Curtis, Revs. T. Stevens, D. M. Graham and others assisting in the exercises. His Honor, the Mayor, and the City Government of Dover were in attendance, and escorted to the place of burial the procession, consisting of the relatives of the deceased, the Corporators of the Printing Establishment, the employees of the *Star* office, the members of the Foreign Mission Board, the Board of Directors of Strafford Bank, the Freewill Baptist ministers in attendance, the members of the Washington Street church, and others. The pall bearers were the deacons of the several evangelical churches in Dover. The places of business in the city were closed between the hours of ten and three, and numerous other marks of respect were shown by the citizens. The attendance of strangers from abroad was large. The remains were deposited in the beautiful Pine Hill Cemetery, beside those of the six children who had preceded him to the spirit world.

———

To the memory of Mr. Burr there have been numerous and touching tributes. To the presentation of some of the more important of these tributes the remainder of these pages will be devoted. On the week following that of his death, the *Star* gave the following summary of his labors and estimate of his character. Though written but a day or two subsequent to his death, the statement is very complete as well as brief. In this place, it may serve not only as a tribute to his memory, but also as a statement of what he was and did :

"WILLIAM BURR.

The announcement contained in our last issue, that he whose name stands at the head of this article had gone to the spirit land, carried sorrow to many a heart. Well it might, for his death was not only sudden and unexpected, but the deceased also belonged to the highest type of man; his very name was a synonym for all that pertained to moral and Christian excellence, and such were his relations and responsibilities that it seemed impossible for him to be spared.

Born in Hingham, Mass., June 22d, 1806; went to Boston at the age of fifteen to learn the printer's trade; commenced the printing of *The Morning Star* at Limerick, Me., in May, 1826; converted and joined the Freewill Baptist church in Limerick in 1828; married to Miss Frances McDonald of Limerick the same year; removed to Dover in 1833, and became a member of the 1st Freewill Baptist church; chosen Agent of the Printing Establishment and Editor of the *Star* in 1835; chosen deacon of the Washington Street church at its organization in 1840; held also various other positions of honor and trust in both church and state ; died of apoplexy, Nov. 5, 1866, aged 60 years, 4 months, and 13 days.

Such is a brief outline of the leading events of his life, but they of themselves give us a very inadequate idea of its inner history and true character. These are a study, and a proper delineation of them must be the work of labor and time. He who shall thoroughly accomplish it, will be amply rewarded in the many things which he will behold to love and admire. There will be the kind husband and father, the agreeable companion, the generous and patriotic citizen, the prompt and accurate business man, the able editor, the wise counselor, the friend of the needy and oppressed ; and above all the sincere and earnest Christian. A life-long student, his information was varied and accurate, and his experience large and rich. If he was cautious in arriving at conclusions, those once formed were held most firmly. While he was conservative in his feelings, no man ever put his shoulder to the wheel of progress more resolutely, especially when he was convinced what progress was. He hated evil in all its forms with intensity, and fought it with determination. The wicked feared him, the good loved him, and all respected him.

Religion was the governing principle of his life, and, as such, regulated all his acts. Apart from his duties to his family, there were two enterprises, to promote which his time and attention were largely, and we may say almost solely, devoted, and with the history of which that of his life is closely interwoven. We refer to the

Printing Establishment and the Washington St. church. These were objects which lay very near his heart. He witnessed the birth and growth of each, and while he labored for, and rejoiced in, their prosperity, he felt most keenly for them in the periods of their adversity. Their interests were emphatically his interests. He lived to see each of these enterprises a success, and they will continue to be standing monuments to his memory. In the denomination with which he was connected and which he ardently loved, he has won a lasting name and place. In his departure, one has been added to its catalogue of loved and honored dead. Henceforth, while Randall will continue to be spoken of as its founder, Colby and Marks as its leading evangelists, and Hutchins as a specimen of its highest type of piety, BURR will be known as its organizer.

Such is but an imperfect picture of the man whose genial, expressive countenance and noble, manly form we shall see no more. His last counsels have been given, his labors are ended, and he has gone to be with angels, the redeemed, and especially the Saviour whom he so much adored.

Friend, brother, father, noble man and Christian patriot, thou whom we loved and honored in all these relations, we bid thee farewell! Thou hast not lived in vain. We would profit by thy counsels, emulate thy virtues, and shall be more than satisfied if our reward shall approximate to thine. Pure spirit, enjoy thy rest! We hope to join thee."

On the week of Mr. Burr's death, the other papers in the city gave brief reviews of his career, and voiced the sentiment of the community respecting him and his death, and the testimonials from exchanges abroad were many and appreciative.

Numerous letters of sympathy and condolence were written to the widow of the deceased, but as they were designed for her alone, it is hardly to be expected that they will be reproduced here. Some of these letters came from beyond the ocean.

At the meeting of the Corporators of the Printing Establishment, held early in December, a little more than four weeks subsequent to Mr. Burr's death, the following resolutions were unanimously adopted :

"*Whereas*, It has pleased God to remove by sudden death our honored and beloved fellow-laborer, WILLIAM BURR, ESQ., who has served for more than thirty years as the Agent of the Freewill Baptist Printing Establishment and the Editor of *The Morning Star*, therefore,

Resolved, That it is with profound gratitude for his long and eminent services, and with profound grief over the loss which his departure occasions, that we express our submission to that Providence which smites us, and record our testimony to the worth and usefulness of our departed brother.

Resolved, That we recognize in our deceased associate, qualities of mind and heart such as combined to make him the true Christian man, the warm - hearted friend, the wise counselor, the vigilant guardian of trusts, the skillful and discreet manager of business, and the embodiment of conscientiousness and integrity in his dealings with all men.

Resolved, That, in the peculiarly responsible, difficult and delicate position which he has so long occupied as the Agent of the Printing Establishment and Editor of *The Morning Star*, we have found in him the happy union of hopefulness and caution, patience and energy, conciliation and firmness; showing a ready deference to the opinions of others while maintaining fidelity to his own personal convictions; developing a careful regard for the general good while sacredly recognizing the rights and interests of the individual; at once exhibiting self - sacrifice and maintaining self - respect; never forgetting what was due to a true expediency but always clinging fast to moral principle; forever discharging his duties to men under the sense of responsibility to God; identifying himself with the interests of the Establishment and rejoicing in the prosperity which his labors brought to it, and yet satisfied only when it was serving the cause of spiritual religion; joyfully spending and being spent for the good of his own denomination, but happy in its successes chiefly because he believed they were aiding to bring in the final triumph of the kingdom of God; gaining in honor and esteem as his abilities became recognized and his efficiency became embodied in results, and yet growing in Christian humility and devotion as his life wore on; gathering a rare enjoyment in the circles of earthly life which he lighted with his chastened cheerfulness, and yet ever looking forward and upward to the immortal sphere as the only complete home of his heart. We mourn his loss, but revere his memory; we deplore the sinking of our strength when his arm was so suddenly palsied, but are stirred to higher effort by his abiding example; we would gladly have wrought with him for the achievement of yet other objects, but, aided by God's blessing, we will endeavor to carry forward to completeness the work which he passes over to our hands at the end of so consecrated and efficient a service.

Resolved, That we tender our earnest Christian sympathies to the family and the numerous friends of our deceased brother, and commend them in their affliction to the richest consolations of our Father in heaven."

Resolutions were also passed by Quarterly Meetings located in all parts of the denomination, expressive of Mr. Burr's worth of character, the value of his services to the denomination, the loss sustained by it in his death, and extending

sympathy to his bereaved family. The Yearly
Meetings, in due time, passed resolutions of the
same purport.

The General Conference, at its session held at
Buffalo in Oct., 1868, through its Committee on
the Printing Establishment, said :

"This General Conference having experienced
since its last session a great bereavement in the
death of the late WILLIAM BURR, who for more
than thirty years acted as Editor of the *Morning
Star* and Agent and Treasurer of the Printing
Establishment, does hereby enter upon its records
a grateful recognition of the fidelity, ability, and
signal success with which he discharged the duties
connected with those perplexing and responsible
duties until the close of his life."

In accordance with a previous vote of the Corporators, the Printing Establishment had early in
Oct., 1867, erected a Monument over the grave of
Mr. Burr in Pine Hill Cemetery. It is of marble,
with a base of granite, standing twelve feet high,
measured from the ground, chaste and simple in
design, beautiful indeed but without ostentation,
and so harmonizing with the character and life

which it is erected to commemorate. On the west, or front face, is the following inscription :

WILLIAM BURR

DIED

Nov. 5, 1866,

Æ 60.

This Monument, erected by the
Freewill Baptist Denomination,
stands as a tribute to his memory.

He had charge of the Printing
Office at its opening in 1826,
and was Editor of the Morning Star
and Agent of the Printing
Establishment during a period
of more than thirty years.

(*North Side.*)

By his integrity in business,
his urbanity in social intercourse,
his broad and philanthropic
sympathies, and especially by his
devout earnestness as a Christian,
he won and retained the high
esteem of all who knew him.

He was a member of the City
Government in Dover, and of the
Legislature of New Hampshire ; and
for more than twenty - five
consecutive years was elected
Treasurer of the Benevolent Societies.

" The memory of the just is blessed."

It was dedicated on the 8th of October, in connection with the Anniversaries which convened in Dover on that day. After singing and prayer, addresses were made to a large assemblage of people by Rev. H. Quinby and Rev. E. Knowlton. The first recalled incidents in the early life and associations of Mr. Burr, and the second spoke of some of the leading traits of his character as a business man and Christian. In the evening a Eulogy was pronounced upon the character and services of Mr. Burr by Rev. G. T. Day, D. D., in the Washington Street church. It occupied about an hour and a quarter in delivery, and was regarded as one of the author's best efforts. From a production so full of brilliant and excellent passages, it is difficult to make a selection, but perhaps no extract can more appropriately appear at this place in this volume than the following, which relates to the service which Mr. Burr rendered the denomination :

"Of his work for us as a Christian denomination it would be easy and pleasant for us to speak freely ; but it may be too soon to estimate that properly, and a few words will be better than many. That work was a needed and peculiar one, and it was large, important, interested, laborious, — a work prompted and sustained by love and distinguished by fidelity. He felt both

the privilege and responsibility of his position and
his service. He had many cares, anxieties and
trials in connection with his service, as every real,
useful, responsible worker must have. He came
to us when we were weak and unorganized; he
helped us into strength and unity. He came to
fill a sphere for which we had no fitted occupant;
he filled and then enlarged it, growing himself as
the functions increased their proportions, —
managing an institution which began in debt to
the amount of half its value, and providing for a
steady prosperity which has made it a growing
bond of union, a medium for the effective exercise
of our power, and a scatterer of benefactions
which have fallen in abundant blessing from the
valley of the Mississippi to the shore of the
Ganges. Few men would have brought to his
task among us so true a heart and so free a service as he laid down through so many years at our
feet; and few could have done for us so ample
and fitting a work, even if they had possessed his
rare and unselfish devotion. He was identified
with us as a people scarcely less closely than with
his own family; and next to his love for them
was his abounding affection for us. He was a
good and discreet manager; — a balance-wheel
that kept our ecclesiastical machinery steady in
its movement without taxing our motive power; —
successful in harmonizing conflicting interests and
opinions; — blending firmness and conciliation; —
knowing when to resist innovation, and yet
yielding without bitterness and after-complaint
to what was a decisive verdict; — not daringly

and audaciously attempting to lead the body on the one hand, nor reluctantly dragged onward by its providential momentum on the other, he generally marched abreast with its best sentiment as did Mr. Lincoln with the nation; giving it his sympathy, keeping its confidence, growing in its esteem, and himself lifted into higher hope and nobler moral stature by the reciprocal blessing which the denomination poured back into the spirit of its benefactor."

To the above the following may be added, which is designed to convey the great lesson of his life:

"Here was a man without brilliance of parts, without unusual opportunities or marked abilities, inheriting no fortune, helped by no influential friends, having at least his full share of hardship and discouragement, sharing nothing of what men call good luck, amid unpromising surroundings, lifted to no eminent station, gaining nothing save what he honestly earns by persistent and taxing industry, taking every ascending step up the hill of difficulty, and living by his labor whose common implements he never lays down to the end of his life. He is a fair example of our common lot and life; he springs from the people and is eminently one of the people; he shares their common hardships and carries their common burdens; he has only the helps and resources which are their usual inheritance, and no grander career is opened before him by Providence than is opened to them. IIe starts from only the average level of American citizenship, and he is supplied with simply the usual stimulants. And in what he became and in what he·did—in his industry, his economy, his integrity, his acquired ability and skill, his study and growth in knowledge, his Christian virtues, his official positions, the growing confidence which he inspired, the increasing influence which he wielded in a whole denomination, the strong friendships which he won, the prayers that were daily offered for him in a thousand homes, the eagerness with which men sought his counsel, the deference paid to his opinions, the grief and tears which burst forth when he fell, the spontaneous standing still of business with uncovered head when his body went by on its way to the grave, the crystallization of religious esteem into a shaft of marble which you have just left standing above his dust to speak your thought of him to the future, this gathering here to - night that you may lay your tribute on the altar that guards his memory,—in all these things we have but so many indications of what a common lot and life may be when the highest duties are honored, and God has put the crown of his waiting favor upon the loyal and loving soul."

As an appropriate close of these tributes to the memory of Mr. Burr and of this volume, the following poem written for the *Star* by Mrs. V. G. Ramsey, whose poetical talent Mr. Burr held in high esteem, is here presented :

THE UNFORGOTTEN DEAD.

TO THE MEMORY OF WILLIAM BURR.

Prized weekly visitant, thou bringest ever
  A welcome presence to my waiting heart,
A memory dear of one whose spirit never
  Seems from thy pages and thy work apart.

I know full well, beyond the pearly portal,
  Which shuts the Golden City from our eyes,
Forever blest, he dwells with the immortal,
  Where beauty never fades nor friendship dies.

And yet, so deeply is his memory graven,
  Time has no power the record to efface;
His influence lives with us, the while in heaven
  He sees the glories of Jehovah's face.

For with a patient zeal and love untiring,
  He labored faithfully through good and ill;
Asking not honor, nor to wealth aspiring,
  He sought alone to do the Master's will.

With lamp all burning and his sheaves around him,
  He heard the midnight cry the Bridegroom
    sends,—
The summons came unheralded, but found him
  Robed for the feast where Jesus meets his friends.

And when, with sorrowing hearts and tearful faces,
  We heard the tidings that his work was done,
We said, "the Father to his own embraces
  Has called the servant whom his grace has won."

O gracious Lord, beneath thy wing abiding,
  And closely pressing to thy wounded side,
Help us, with patient trust and love confiding,
  To do thy will though good or ill betide.

So may we hope, when this brief life is over,
  And all the work thou givest us is done,
That thou, O Jesus! pitying Friend and Brother,
  Wilt crown us with the joys which he has won.